The Heart's Return

A CHRISTMAS NOVELLA

THE WHINBURG TOWNSHIP AMISH
BOOK TEN

ADINA SENFT

First published in *Amish Christmas Miracles*, November 2020. Cover design by Moonshell Books, Inc. using images under license. Translation of the German by the author.

The Heart's Return / Adina Senft—2nd ed.

ISBN 978-1-963929-21-8 R091924

 Created with Vellum

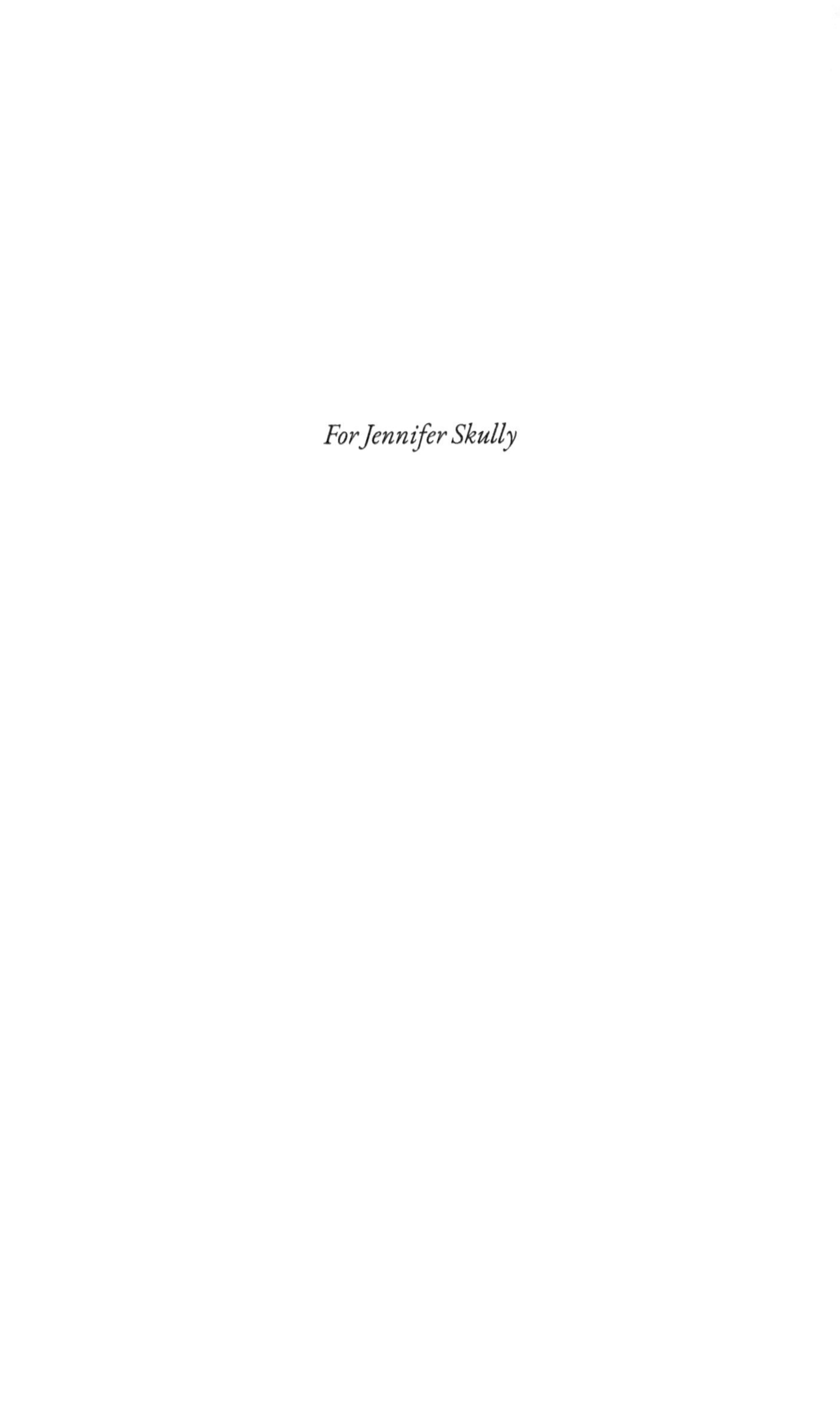

For Jennifer Skully

The Heart's Return

Chapter One

WHINBURG TOWNSHIP, PENNSYLVANIA

Ten days before Christmas

Anna Esch set her mother's clay pitcher in the center of the tiny kitchen table and stood back to admire it. In the summer, *Mamm* had always put flowers in it, but this close to Christmas, Anna had carried on the tradition by picking sprigs of holly and some evergreens, and arranging them until the cheerful combination of red and green pleased her. For Anna, *Mamm*'s pitcher was the last thing that made their new house a home.

Then she braced her hands on her back to stretch the kinks out of it. How was it possible for two people to move such a short distance—just across the yard—and yet it be so much work?

But then, half of the work had been sorting, throwing away, and boxing things up for the Mennonite charity, not actually moving. They'd left the furniture in the big house, because it would never fit here in the *Daadi Haus*. Anna and *Dat* had brought their own beds and mattresses and all the quilts. But would she ever get over feeling that this was her grandmother's kitchen, not hers? That she wasn't really supposed to sit on *Mammi*'s sofa—brand new in 1994—in case she got mud on it?

The window over the sink looked across the yard to the big house, where an *Englisch* box van, a spring wagon, and a gray-sided buggy were all in various stages of being unloaded. Thank goodness the Bontragers had a dry week for a move. It felt like snow today, though. There was a waiting quality to the air. A kind of expectant silence. By morning they might have an inch ... or a foot.

But by morning, Lester and Eva Bontrager would be all moved into the house that Anna had called home all her life. Something caught in her chest—a hitch that felt almost like grief. But how could it be? She and *Dat* were incredibly fortunate that they'd found not only excellent tenants, but tenants who were also old friends. Eva and *Mamm* had been friends while *Mamm* was alive, and now that their family was grown, they had come back to the township to farm. Lester, it seemed, liked a challenge. And the Esch farm was certainly that.

The back door opened, and Anna swallowed down her foolish emotions. A female voice said, "Brrr!" She stamped her feet. "Anna? *Bischt du hier?*"

"Ja," she said. Of course she was here. Where else would she be if she was no longer in the big house? "Come on in. It's taken me until now to fill the cupboards and pantry, but I'm finished. The coffee is on."

Rubber boots thumped on the mat, a coat rustled as it was hung on the peg, and then her married sister Lizzie came in on a breath of cold air, holding a plastic cake carrier. "Oh good, you've got *Mamm*'s pitcher out. I always liked it."

Anna knew that, but she wasn't about to suggest Lizzie take it home with her. Lizzie had so much—a devoted, hardworking husband, a nice home where they were to have church this Sunday, and two adorable girls and a boy that were the light of Anna's life. Lizzie and Byron lived just over the creek on the neighboring farm, and they saw each other almost daily.

Anna would keep the pitcher. It was little enough.

Lizzie put the rectangular plastic container on the counter. "I brought you a gingerbread cake as a housewarming present. I didn't think you'd have time to bake today, and it's Christmassy." She adjusted her *Kapp* on her dark hair, tightened the bow in its strings on her chest as though they might have loosened on the walk over, and glanced around the kitchen. "It looks just the same. Are you using *Mammi*'s dishes?"

"No, I brought *Mamm*'s," Anna said. "Do you want the old ones?"

Lizzie shook her head. "What would I do with them? I got all new ones for wedding gifts. They'll do for years yet. Is that coffee ready? Shall I cut the cake?"

Anna had to smile. "Probably and *ja. Denki*, Lizzie. It was kind of you."

"If Eva and Lester and all the helpers are coming over for dinner, you'll need it." Lizzie found the knife drawer by memory and slid the cake out of the container. "I made one for her, too, but I'll wait a little. It looks pretty busy over there. I don't want to get in the men's way."

Lizzie's gingerbread cake with the brown-sugar frosting was the perfect antidote for a difficult day.

Lizzie poured them both a cup of hot coffee, then took the pot back to the stove. "I felt badly about not being able to help you move," she said, sitting down. "But with Byron's niece's wedding tomorrow, church at our place Sunday, and Christmas the Friday after that, I've been cleaning and cooking from dawn until dusk. More than usual, I mean. A trainload of Byron's sisters and cousins have helped with the cleaning, or I'd never have finished. They're all here for the wedding, of course. I will be so glad when it's all over and we can get back to normal."

Normal. Anna stopped herself from gazing out the window in the direction of the house.

"Whatever possessed Lester and Eva to move in this week, of all weeks?" Lizzie said on a sigh. "Not that I'm not glad to see them."

Anna nodded. "We can't expect them to schedule their lives to make ours more convenient," she said. "I'm glad they're here too. They can spend Christmas with all of us, and maybe not feel so homesick for Bucks County. Lester has lots of plans for the farm."

"It will take a heap of work to get this farm in good order again." Lizzie sipped her coffee. "Much as we both love *Dat*..." Her voice trailed away before she said the truth out loud.

But there was no escaping it. The farm had become more and more run down over the nearly eleven years since his parents had died and he'd inherited it. Seed had rotted in unprepared fields. Cows had sickened on moldy silage. He had done his best, but with no sons to work the farm and his three daughters' help not enough, it had gotten away from him. The simple fact was that, much as he wanted to be, *Dat* was not the best provider in the world, but not for lack of trying. He loved his children, and they loved him, but only the spirit could live on love. The body had to be supported somehow. They were only here because of the charity of the church, the extra work of the men of the *Gmee* lending a hand, and *Mamm* and Anna's garden . . . which, Anna supposed, would be Eva's when spring came. If it hadn't been for her brother-in-law Byron's kindness in leasing the two fields closest to his own, and the letter from Lester Bontrager inquiring about leasing the rest of the farm, Anna couldn't imagine where they'd be. It was sure and certain that *Dat*'s birdhouses wouldn't pay the mortgage he'd had to take out to keep the farm going, especially since half the time he gave them away to the children in the market who admired them.

"Oh, I know what I meant to tell you," Lizzie said suddenly, interrupting Anna's reverie. "I was over at *Englisch* Henry Byler's getting some elderberry syrup from Sarah for Daniel's cough. She told me that Eva said they were expecting more company before Christmas. Maybe even in time for Sunday."

"Already?" Anna said in surprise. "Why, they'll barely have their boxes open or a place to sit, never mind beds made up and food cooked. I'd better ask Eva if she can use a hand. Do we know who's coming?"

Lizzie nodded and swiped a piece of frosting off the cake plate. "It's not a crowd. Just her brother. You remember, he moved away years ago. Just before I was married."

Anna went still, her breathing halting altogether.

"Not that I'd have looked at him then—I wanted Byron to drive me home from singing. I was a woman on a mission, though of course Byron didn't know that. Oh, what was his name?"

Breathe. "The older brother?" she managed. "Or the younger?"

"Eva has a bunch of brothers. It's hard to tell them apart. The one that went to Colorado."

"Neil." Anna could hardly get the name out. "The youngest."

Lizzie nodded. "That's right. Neil Wengerd. I wonder if he made anything of himself? Poor boy, there was nothing on the family place for him. Divide it up any more and no one would be able to work it. That's the trouble with the farms here. Land is so expensive, and you have to keep the acres together. The old ways of dividing them up among sons just don't work in this day and age. Not when a man still has to provide for a wife and family. No wonder more of our boys are going to work in the RV factories and the like."

But Anna didn't want to talk about farms and factories. She wanted to run up to her room and lie on her bed and cry. And then pray to *der Himmlischer Vater* to help her find her peace again.

Eventually Lizzie left, taking her plastic container with her. Anna did the dishes and put them away. A glance at the clock told her she'd better get supper going, since *Dat* would be home any minute, and Eva and Lester and the moving crew would be here at five o'clock.

She was just stirring mushroom soup into the hamburger for the pizza casserole when a terrible thought immobilized her, the wooden spoon motionless in her hand.

What if Neil were here already? What if he had come, and already joined the crew that was taking things in and out, and she just didn't know it? What if he was coming for supper, too?

Neh. Anna shook her head and began to scrape the bits off the bottom of the cast-iron frying pan.

She'd have known it—felt it—if he were here, so close.

So close ... and for eight years now, farther away than he had ever been.

"THAT WAS A FINE MEAL, *DOCHSDER*." Anna's father, Wilmer Esch, leaned back in his chair and patted his stomach. "I've always said you'll make a fine wife for a good man someday. But I hope the Lord doesn't will it too soon!"

Anna could have sunk through the plank floor with mortification as their company laughed. At twenty-seven years old, she'd already turned the first corner. Any day now, the women of Willow Creek would be suggesting she attend the "senior singles" quilting frolics and help her to find the widowers looking for mothers for their children.

The guests at their table—Eva and Lester, one of her older brothers and his teenage boys, Rafe and Elmer—thanked her for the meal. At least now was a good time to busy herself putting on the coffee and clearing the table for dessert. Eva got up to help, and later, after the gingerbread cake had been demolished and *Dat* had taken the men out to show them his workshop, she and her new neighbor settled in the *Daadi Haus*'s tiny sitting room.

"This seems very snug," Eva said, looking about her with a smile.

Anna had always appreciated that about Neil's older sister —she had the gift of contentment. Of course, she made no secret of the fact that whithersoever Lester was, there she would be also, and that was the source of much of her happiness. Oh, if the *gut Gott* would only send such a match for Anna!

"It is," she replied, stifling the longing that rose up inside her. "*Dat* sleeps downstairs, and I have my room upstairs, plus a small room for my sewing and my books. We will manage just fine without five bedrooms and living rooms big enough to seat the whole *Gmee*."

Space was a requirement in an Amish home. If the house couldn't accommodate the church when it was that family's turn to host it, then a barn or equipment shed would do. God came first. And that meant service in the form of building a home large enough for the Holy Spirit to bring the *Gmee* together in worship every other Sunday.

"I look forward to having church here," Eva said with a smile. "I admit the house is more than we need, now that our youngest is married and the other four have their own homes, but they'll all be coming for visits, and I'll be glad of it then. Your father settled on rent that we can afford, so we took it as a sign that God wanted us here again."

"Lester is happy to be back in Whinburg Township?" Anna said, hesitant to make any reference to the past.

Who remembered anymore that Neil Wengerd had once courted her? Not even Lizzie, and that was saying something. But still, this was Neil's sister.

"*Ja*, he is," Eva said fondly. "We were newlyweds here, and we both have family in the township. He can't wait to get his hands into Whinburg soil again. So as long as your father is willing to rent to us, we're glad to stay and put down roots." She sighed. "I wish my brother Neil could find the place God wants him. You remember Neil?"

"*Ja*," Anna said. The word rasped from a throat suddenly dry. She took a sip of her coffee.

"He's coming for Christmas, which makes me so happy. A new home with old memories, and my brother here as well to make more." She smiled at the doorway, as though he might walk through it at any moment. "It's a little Christmas miracle that he could come at all. He's been very successful out there in Colorado, and it's difficult to get away."

"Oh?" Anna tried not to look as though she was hanging on every word. But of course, she was.

"Yes. He's in Westcliffe, you know, in the Wet Mountain Valley."

"Is it wet?" Anna joked feebly.

"In the winter it can be. Mountain ranges on either side and only a three-month growing season, Neil says. So he chose not to farm. He bought into a buffalo ranch, of all things, and is the foreman there. Can you imagine it? He manages buffalo the way the rest of us keep cows!"

Anna's mouth fell open as she tried to picture such a thing. "Buffalo," she said at last. "Like on a nickel."

"Exactly." Eva nodded. "Don't let this get out, but apparently their biggest customers are movie people filming westerns and things. He doesn't have anything to do with them, mind you, but since he owns a share, he gets part of that money. And believe me, he says it's a lot."

It was like hearing about someone she'd never met. Someone who would never be closer than a story told around the dinner table, to shakes of the head and whistles of amazement that such time-wasters as movies could produce real money to live on.

Steps clumped across the front porch, and someone knocked on the door.

"Who could that be?" Eva said. "All my menfolk are with your father, aren't they?"

"It could be my sister Lizzie," Anna said, crossing the worn carpet to the door. "She made a gingerbread cake for a housewarming present for you and said she'd bring it over."

As she opened the door, she was still smiling at the way Eva leaped from the chair at the prospect of that cake. Snowflakes danced in on the cold, landing on Anna's cheeks and heart-shaped *Kapp*.

But she didn't feel them. Her spirit seemed to have left her body, rising up in a great, silent shout of shock and joy as her wide-eyed gaze met his.

"Guder owed, Anna," said Neil Wengerd. "Looks like I went to the wrong house. Is my sister here?"

Chapter Two

Time seemed to telescope out and race past, all at the same time. Eva descended upon her brother with hugs and exclamations, and the next thing Anna knew, she had carried him away to the big house, and *Dat* had come in to say that everyone had gone home.

Fifteen words.

All that time away, and when he'd seen her again, he'd given her only fifteen words. But oh, his voice, rippling over the syllables of her name in that way only he had. Had he meant to say it so? Or was it thoughtless, accidental? And his eyes! The blue of a September morning, framed in dark lashes, lowered a little as he looked down into her face.

A face that had probably been all too easy to read. A face that had likely shown him how much her regret had cost her every day of the eight years since they'd seen each other last. Since her mother had gotten sick and her parents had convinced her to turn him down because she was so young—he was so poor—they needed her so much. Her guilt and unworthiness at misleading him about it to keep *Mamm*'s secret haunted her still—especially when, heartbroken and angry, he'd gone away.

After a sleepless night, she hauled herself out of bed to make *Dat* his breakfast. Out in the barn afterward, she fed the chickens, some of whom were still on their roosts, fluffed up to keep themselves warm until the sun came up. Would Eva take over this job now or allow Anna to care for them as she'd always done? Maybe when it came time to put the non-layers in the freezer they rented in Willow Creek, she'd leave that job to Eva. She loved the chickens, and even though part of their purpose was to feed the family, she'd always hated having to force them to their sacrifice.

When she came out of the barn, in the distance she heard the commotion of the first buggies rolling in for Byron's niece's wedding. She could also hear the phone ringing in *Dat*'s workshop behind the barn. There was no answering machine, so a caller would let it ring for a long time in case someone had to run for it. She counted a dozen rings before she was close enough to push open the door and pick up the receiver, answering it breathlessly.

"Hallo, Anna," said Malinda Kanagy in her calm way. *She* probably never ran for the telephone. Her callers would always wait. "It's Malinda. *Wie geht's?*"

"I'm very well. People are beginning to arrive next door for the wedding. Are you coming?"

"Ja," Malinda said. "The bride and I are in the same buddy bunch. *Dat* is just hitching up. Say, before you go over, I wonder if you could pass on a message to Neil Wengerd?"

She already knew he was here? How was that possible?

As though that tiny hitch of silence had communicated Anna's surprise, Malinda said, "We were coming home from my aunt and uncle's and saw him at the Whinburg bus station. He hasn't changed a bit. *Dat* recognized him right away and offered him a ride. It was nice to catch up after all this time."

Malinda Kanagy had had the privilege of seeing him first, of catching up on all his news. Malinda, who had probably not given him a single thought in eight years. While she, Anna, would have treasured every word as though it were an apple of gold in a frame of silver. "I'd be happy to give him a message," she finally said, doing her best to sound as if this were not an opportunity straight from the hand of God.

"I told him that singing is at our place Friday, but I forgot to say that some of the boys will be having a pond hockey game before supper, while there's enough light. Lots of the *Youngie* will be staying over after the wedding. Neil probably doesn't have skates, but I'm sure someone will have an extra pair."

How strange that after all they had been to one another, Anna didn't know if Neil even liked pond hockey. "I'll be sure to tell him."

"You're very welcome to come, too, Anna. I haven't seen you at a singing in a little while, and it would be fun. Dress warmly. *Dat* has promised us a bonfire, but if it keeps snowing like this, he might decide against it."

"*Denki,*" Anna said. "It's pretty busy around here, though, with two households moving and the wedding on top of it. And *Dat* only has me."

"You need fellowship too," Malinda said. "And there's nothing wrong with a bit of fun."

"I'll do my best." Wouldn't that start a rumor among the younger set? *Anna Esch hasn't been to a singing in ages, and the moment Neil Wengerd turns up, there she is, making moony eyes at him across the table.*

"See you then," Malinda said. "Bye."

Anna hung up slowly and set off along the path through the dormant garden. To say more than three sentences to Neil. She must pull her courage around her like a warm coat and use it to protect her heart. Because he should not see anything in her face but friendliness and hospitality.

One of his cousins told her she could find him in the barn, and there he was, cleaning the Bontrager buggy of its mud and travel dust. Clearly, they weren't planning on going to the wedding. He straightened as he saw her and wiped his hands with his rag.

"Hallo, Anna. This is a surprise."

"We only live across the yard," she said. "And our chickens are in the back, there, out of the cold. I'm in and out of this barn a lot."

"I meant—"

"I was just talking to Malinda Kanagy," she went on in as steady a voice as she could manage. Polite. Friendly. "She says that before the singing at their place on Friday, some of the boys are getting up a pond hockey game. You're welcome to join them."

"Oh," he said, as though he'd been expecting her to give a different message altogether from Malinda. Something more personal, maybe?

"She says that if you don't have skates, one of the boys will probably have an extra pair."

"I don't have skates," he said. "Not the first thing I thought about packing into my single bag for my trip across the country."

"*Ja.* Well. Anyway, the offer is there." She turned to go.

"Anna, wait." He came out from behind the buggy, and a

flash of memory ambushed her. How tall he was. How she'd had to stretch up on tiptoe for a kiss good night. How she'd thought that every kiss for the rest of her life would be his alone. And how happy that had made her.

Wasted kisses, they'd turned out to be. How many had he given to other girls, out there in Colorado?

"Are you going?" he asked.

She flushed at her treacherous thoughts. "To the wedding? Of course."

"*Neh*, to the singing Friday. At the Kanagys." He sounded as patient as a schoolteacher.

"Oh. I—I don't know."

"I thought you would be. You always used to."

Because he would be there. Because he would give her a ride home, and they would talk far into the night before Star, his horse, fell asleep on her feet. She looked forward to Fridays the way *Mamm* had used to look forward to the first crocuses in the garden. As though it were the only thing that would get her through the winter.

"I don't go so much. *Mamm* passed away, you know, and with Lizzie busy with her own family and my oldest sister on her husband's farm in Smicksburg, *Dat* only has me to look after him."

"But will you go Friday?"

Was he just asking to make conversation? Or did he want her to be there?

"Malinda invited me specially, so I probably will," she said at last. "You should invite your cousins, too. Everyone will be glad to see them." Especially Malinda's younger sister Rosanne, who ran with a crowd of seventeen-year-olds all in a hurry to be grown up enough to date.

"We could all go together," he suggested. "Lester won't mind if I borrow the buggy. With Rafe and Elmer and me, that leaves a seat empty."

Oh, no. She was not about to arrive at singing with a buggy full of young men, all of whom were single, one of whom she had once believed she would marry. No, no, no. Not only would she be seen as fast—laughable thought, at her age!—but it would bring back far too many memories.

"*Denki*, but I'll probably walk. The Kanagys are just across the west field from Lizzie. The pond is down in that little dip between."

"But—"

"As long as we don't have a blizzard between now and Friday, it will be fine." She risked a smile. "Bye, now. I need to change my clothes and get to the wedding."

"Anna—hey—"

But she made a clean escape. And he didn't come after her.

THE WEDDING of Byron's niece went off without a hitch. To Anna's deep gratitude, the bride was too young to know her well and so forgot to make arrangements for a young man to sit with Anna at supper, leaving her free to serve the guests while Lizzie's daughters served the newlywed couple in the *Eck*, the beautifully decorated corner table. Wednesday morning, the bride and groom set off on their honeymoon visits to relatives in Lancaster County, and the cleanup over at Lizzie's took until midafternoon. The bench wagon was packed up and driven off to the next wedding, which was Thursday, and from there it would come back to Lizzie's for church on Sunday. Amanda

Yoder's wedding was on the Tuesday before Christmas. Her intended, Joshua King, and his family would be staying at *Englisch* Henry and Sarah Byler's over the holy day, and then Amanda would travel back to Colorado with them all to begin her new life there.

Would Neil travel back with them? Anna wondered as she put on her coat Friday night, preparing to go to the singing. It made sense that he would. He probably fellowshipped with them—after all, there were only two churches in the Westcliffe district.

With a sigh, Anna pulled on her snow boots, tucked her house shoes into a canvas tote along with a bean salad, tied the ribbons tight on her away bonnet, and wrapped her scarf around her throat and up over her nose and cheeks.

When she came down the steps, the boys were climbing into the buggy so that Eva could settle what looked like a casserole dish on one of their laps. When she caught sight of Anna, she hurried over.

"Neil tells me you're going to walk. Anna, I forbid it. You go with the boys. The thermometer says it's twenty degrees!"

"*Neh,* I—"

"No arguments. There's a seat free and a nice wool blanket. No one in their right mind would think anything of your going in the buggy when it's this cold. Come along now. In you get."

It would be far more embarrassing to refuse than it would to arrive at the Kanagys' with a bunch of young men. Anna had no choice. With a nod and a smile, she climbed up on the empty seat on the left, next to Neil, who was driving. Eva slid the door shut with the sound of finality. "Have fun!"

Even if Anna had had the courage to speak up and talk to him, his nephews left her no chance. They chattered like a pair of spring robins all the way to the Kanagy farm, and even Neil couldn't get a word in edgewise. On the good side, she managed to slip out of the buggy unseen by anyone except her companions, because a buggy filled with the young men from Colorado as well as Simon Yoder, the *Dokterfraa*'s son, arrived at the same time, and everyone's attention swung to the strangers.

"Can I carry that in for you?" Neil said in a low voice as he joined her beside Lester's horse, Jubilee. He reached up to pat the horse's neck. "Then I'll put this good boy in the barn."

"*Neh, denki,*" she said. "Best get him in before he gets a chill."

"Will you come and watch the hockey game?"

"Maybe," she said. "Are you going to find a pair of skates?"

"Sure. I can keep warm better if I'm moving. I'd forgotten how different the cold is here."

"How is it different?" she asked in spite of herself. That was something she'd never considered. Then again, she'd never been farther from home than Smicksburg, at the other end of the state.

"It's dry."

"It's dry here in the winter too." *Mamm* used to have to use eyedrops because the winter air dried out her eyes sometimes.

"Really dry, and at seven thousand feet, the altitude can make newcomers sick. When you step off the train, your nostrils pinch together with the cold."

"My goodness." Were they really reduced to discussing the weather, after all they'd once been? "I'd best get in the house. Have fun."

If she stood here another second, she would cry at the loss of the intimacy they'd known. Not physical, but a kind of emotional intimacy. Private jokes. Soft asides that only the other heard. Long conversations by lamplight where each had complete freedom of spirit. Freedom to be honest about their hopes, their dreams.

By the time she reached the house, removed her boots and bonnet, and had pulled her scarf through the sleeve of her coat so it wouldn't get mixed up with the others piled on the bed, she'd regained control of herself. With such a houseful expected and Malinda and Rosanne down at the pond, their mother was only too glad of Anna's help. She kept quietly busy, even when everyone finally trooped in for supper, red-cheeked and laughing, snow melting on eyebrows and hems and socks.

But Anna wasn't so busy that she missed the way a seat magically opened up next to Malinda Kanagy at supper and Neil Wengerd took it with a smile. She tried not to watch them talking together, Malinda's pretty face lighting up with amusement as he told her a funny story—about the buffalo? Or about cowboys? There were cowboys in Colorado, weren't there? *Dat* read secondhand Western novels by the shopping-bag full. He would know.

Anna edged closer to hear as the light from the Coleman lamps made the other girl's hair even more golden. Neil had such a protective way of leaning toward a woman, as though he really wanted to hear what she had to say.

Anna had loved that about him. Time was when the things she said had mattered to him. And then those final sentences ... those had mattered most of all. Those had changed their lives and couldn't be taken back, much as she had wept and wanted to. By then, he had left Whinburg Township and taken her heart with him.

"... and before I knew it, the animal had circled back around and was standing right behind me."

"What did you do?" Normally unflappable, Malinda could almost be holding her breath with anticipation.

"Well, turns out buffalo don't see very well. I moved ever so slowly out of its sight line and then got over that fence so fast I lost my hat and split my pants right down the back. The ranch hands had better eyesight than that buffalo and saw the whole thing. I didn't hear the end of it for weeks."

Malinda laughed, and Neil gazed down into her face. Was he wondering how any woman could be so beautiful? The thing was, Malinda always behaved as though she was unaware of her looks. An Amish woman would never be so *batzich* as to say she liked the job God had done. Some homes in the township didn't even have mirrors in them, though Anna had seen girls fixing their hair in front of the glass doors of their mother's china cabinets, struggling to see their reflections. Malinda must know she was pretty, but she was always so humble, so calm, so in control of herself and her emotions. She could cook well, her mother had taught her to manage the home, and her quilts always sold for a high price at the mud sales for the volunteer fire department. Much higher than the ones Anna and Lizzie made.

There was no getting around it. Malinda Kanagy was the catch of the township. Maybe even the county. And Neil was no longer the penniless fourth son. Anna braced herself mentally to hear someone say—maybe even tonight—that *Malinda Wengerd* had a nice ring to it.

Malinda's mother finally told Anna very firmly that she was to stop serving and go and have some supper. Well, she'd put it off as long as she could, and while she didn't have much appetite, she took a plate and helped herself to a chicken and bacon casserole, some of her bean salad, and her favorite baked corn, which Priscilla Mast always brought. It had to be the most fattening thing on the planet, but it was mighty satisfying on a cold night—proved by the fact that she got the very last spoonful in the pan.

Anna found a seat on the far side of the big table, crowded with *Youngie*, and a moment later felt a shock of surprise as Simon Yoder folded himself into the place next to her.

"Hope you don't mind," Simon said, digging in. "Was this seat saved for someone?"

"Not at all," Anna managed after she'd got her hanging jaw to close. "It's a good crowd, isn't it? But then, it usually is during wedding season, with people's families in town."

Simon took a long drink of his soda. "I don't see you much at these things."

Anna resisted the urge to stare at him. He had never dropped more than a sentence in her direction since he'd begun his *Rumspringe* a couple of years ago. She had joined church at twenty, after Neil had gone, and had done hardly any running around at all. "I don't come so much anymore," she said. "It feels different when you're twenty-seven than when you're seventeen."

At seventeen, every singing held the possibility of meeting the boy God had in mind for you. At twenty-seven, you began to wonder if God had no one in mind at all, and simply meant you to be content in the place where you were.

Or God had already shown you His choice, and you had sent him away.

"I'm closer to twenty-seven than seventeen myself," Simon said.

Anna shot him a droll glance. "You are not. You're only twenty-one."

"*Ja*. But sometimes experience can make you feel older than years do." Simon returned her glance without so much as a glint in his brown eyes. "Don't you think?"

Anna lifted a shoulder. "I can't say. I haven't had much experience. Not like you. You and Neil and Amanda have been to Colorado and done things that I could never dream of."

"Why not?"

What did he mean?

"You could go to Colorado, too," he said, in answer to the question clearly in her face. "There isn't as much work in the winter as there is in the summer, but lots of the *Youngie* go in the spring and come back in the fall. There's no reason why you couldn't do that, too."

It was almost as though an earthquake had quietly shaken the ground under her feet. Simon Yoder, of all people, giving her life advice. Whatever next?

"Simon? Anna? Can I take your plates?" Malinda was standing behind their chairs and Anna hadn't even seen her get up.

"*Neh*, let me." Hastily, Anna rose, took the plate that Simon held, and swerved around Malinda, heading for the kitchen the way a hockey player heads for the goal posts on a breakaway.

Of all the strange experiences she'd ever had, this one took the cake. Simon Yoder was the worst flirt in the township, if you asked any of the single girls. He had a sketchy reputation, too. Something had happened out in Colorado that no one wanted to talk about, and this alone would make any Plain girl hesitant to be seen too often in his company.

Now the whole crowd of *Youngie* had seen him singling her out, including Neil Wengerd. Could his timing have been any worse?

At least during the singing, nothing strange was likely to happen. After supper was cleared away and the tables wiped down, the girls sat at one, and the boys the other. As the hostess, Malinda chose the first song—number 70 in the *Ausbund*.

Frölich so will ich singen,
Mit Lust ein Tageweiß,
Von wunderlichen Dingen,
Dem höchsten Gott zu Preiß,
In seinem Namen heb ich an,
Sein Gnad woll er mir günen,
So g'lingt mirs auf der Bahn.

Joyfully I want to sing,
With desire pure as day,
For wonderful and awesome things
The highest God to praise,
In His name I am raised up,
His mercy will he grant
So I'll know victory on the way.

Anna loved music—when others made it. Oh, she could carry a tune in a bucket, just not very far. It wasn't the Amish way to sing in parts during church on a Sunday, but at singing on Friday nights, the *Youngie* often did. She could sing alto if she concentrated, but most of the time she preferred not to draw attention to herself with notes that sounded different from those of her neighbors.

And then ... above the voices with which she was so familiar came a clear soprano, as pure as the song of a lark over the fields. It was Cora Swarey, who had come from Colorado with the family of Amanda's intended. Anna nearly fell silent as she listened, spellbound, to the girl's beautiful voice. It seemed to encourage the others to sing in parts, to try to support the gift of that sound. The boys from Colorado chose bass and tenor, and Anna could distinctly hear Malinda, two places down, singing the alto part. Very well, then. She'd support Malinda and no one would think she was trying to show off.

Anna's heart filled with joy. How *wunderbaar* it was that they could all lift their voices at once in praise, creating a unified sound made up of many individuals. Just the way they would all sing around God's throne in eternity. They sang seven verses of the hymn's twenty-eight. Then, as though to bring them back to earth, someone suggested "Country Roads," and after that "How Great Thou Art," and a mix of country songs, old-fashioned *Englisch* hymns, and newer hymns from the little songbook they sometimes used.

As Anna sang the words so familiar she didn't need to look at them, she happened to see Simon Yoder gazing at Cora as though he were seeing a vision. Which was strange, because to Anna's knowledge, they had gone to church together out there in Colorado, so he already knew her. And then, with a kind of jolt under her breastbone, she realized that Neil Wengerd was also gazing across to the girls' table.

Not at Malinda, as might have been expected, but at her, Anna.

Anna felt the hot burn of a blush rise in her cheeks. She dropped her eyes to her song book once more. He should not see her looking back at him. The days of stealing glances at one another were long over and couldn't be resurrected.

A moment later, her lashes flicked up and then down, just long enough to see that his gaze had moved over to Malinda.

Pain arrowed through her heart. No, it wasn't pain. She'd simply eaten too much supper. That was all. She felt nothing now, and probably neither did he.

Anna focused on the hymn and realized to her chagrin that she'd completely lost her place.

Chapter Three

The next day was Saturday and if there was one thing guaranteed to lift Anna's spirits before Christmas, it was to visit a woman who often tucked her tribulations away under a smile and gave God the praise for her blessings. When Mollie Graber let her in to the basement suite she rented from the trio of Amish sisters who ran the new bakery in Whinburg, Anna folded her into a hug. "How are you feeling?"

"I'm very well, *denki*." Mollie sounded as though she meant it, but Anna could see the lines of pain at the corners of her mouth. She was barely five years older than Anna, but the loss of her husband and only child in a buggy accident, added to crippling arthritis, had robbed her of her youth and bloom. But not of her hope. Nor of her happiness in Anna's visits and the friendship of the sisters upstairs.

"No, truly." Anna set Mollie's walker against the kitchen wall and encouraged her over to the kitchen table. She set down the basket that she had brought, filled with canned peaches, two jars of the raspberry jam that she knew Mollie loved, a loaf of fresh bread, and a casserole that she had made earlier, that could simply be popped into the gas oven and reheated. From under her arm she took a gaily wrapped oblong box with a green bow.

"There are days when I have a lot of pain," Mollie admitted, rubbing her twisted hands. "But the salve that *Englisch* Henry's Sarah gave me has really been helping. She says I'm to rub it in twice a day, and I do believe it's beginning to work. She also said I have to give up eating tomatoes and potatoes. Can you imagine? How could anyone get through a day without either of those?"

"Well, if you don't want to pay the price, it looks like you'll need to. Why those in particular?"

"They're members of the nightshade family, she says. And those can cause inflammation and make the arthritis flare up. Who knows? It may be worth it." Mollie watched Anna put the tea kettle on.

Mollie had been advised by her *Englisch* doctor not to drink coffee, for her heart, and Anna took it as a good sign that she was sticking to that rule. It would certainly be easier for Anna to give up potatoes than coffee.

"Speaking of paying a price, I've been hearing some things about you."

"About me?" Anna never did anything that was remotely gossip-worthy. She hardly ever went out, and when she did, it was only to go to a quilting frolic, or to help someone who needed an extra pair of hands, as Lizzie had during this week's events, or to go to the scratch-and-dent store to pick up bulk groceries. "Who could possibly be talking about me?"

"Well, you know Priscilla Mast comes in once a week as a *Maud*, both upstairs and down here, and this morning she happened to mention how interesting it was that Simon Yoder spent half of supper last night before the singing talking to a certain *Maedel* we both know."

Anna was pretty sure she was past the age where people would refer to her as a *Maedel,* a young girl. "She must have meant Malinda Kanagy." After supper, and before the singing began, Simon had made Malinda laugh with one of his witty stories.

"No, that wasn't the *Maedel* she meant," Mollie said with a smile. "Are you keeping something from your old friend?"

"I am not." Anna gave her a mock stern look. "To tell you the truth, I haven't figured out yet why Simon Yoder would plunk himself down next to me, or why he felt it necessary to start a conversation. We've barely exchanged a word in the last couple of years, not counting the time he's been out in Colorado."

Mollie said nothing, only ran a finger along the smooth length of the green ribbon Anna had tied around the gift.

"Besides, what is it they say? An eavesdropper never learns any good of herself. *Mamm* always told us that when it comes to gossip, a person is likely to learn more about themselves than they are about the person they're speaking of."

"*Ja,* you're right. And so was your *mamm,*" Mollie said. "Though I'm sure the *Dokterfraa* would agree that it's time her boy Simon looked around and got serious about someone who can settle him down. He needs a good woman, with firm princi-ples, who's strong in the faith. A woman like you."

This was so ridiculous that Anna laughed out loud, and Mollie's eyebrows went up. "I'm sorry, *mei freind,*" she said, laying a gentle hand on Mollie's wrist in apology. She couldn't wipe the smile from her face, though. "I'm six years older than

Simon and not exactly the kind of woman that men look at twice. If he were going to chase anyone, it would be Malinda."

"That's the second time you've mentioned her." Mollie never missed anything. "What's going on?"

"Nothing." The kettle boiled, and Anna poured them each a mug of the *Dokterfraa*'s summer tea, fragrant with the scent of grasses and lemon balm. She found some whoopie pies that must have come from upstairs and set them on a plate. Mollie took one as Anna went on, "We all know that she's the catch of the county. I suppose it's natural to speculate that all the men in the township would jump at the chance if she gave them one."

"All the men?" Mollie asked. "I hear there are some new additions from Colorado."

Anna's stomach clenched, and she sipped her tea to hide her expression. Under no circumstances must she betray herself. Mollie's gaze was far too penetrating, and she knew her too well. She had not lived here eight years ago, but that didn't mean she might not have heard a whisper about Anna and Neil in all the time since.

"They seem like good, hardworking young men," Anna said. "And Amanda Yoder looks so happy, she's positively glowing."

"Love will do that for you," Mollie said with a smile. "I remember the days when my late husband and I were courting. They were the happiest of my life." Her smile of remembrance flickered into pain, and she put her mug of tea down carefully. "Why doesn't some discerning man realize what a wonderful wife you would make, Anna?"

"That is in God's hands. He will send the partner He wants me to have. I just have to be patient."

"Maybe, but there's nothing in the Bible that says you can't be out on the road to meet God's choice. Or help Him along."

"Don't you dare go getting ideas," Anna warned her, no longer smiling. "It's bad enough that I heard some of the ladies talking a little too loudly about organizing a *senior singles* frolic. I've already been invited to the widows' quilting frolic next month for the mud sale. If there's anything worse than that, I don't know what it is."

"Not being able to quilt," Mollie said bluntly, rubbing her thumb into her palm. "Be glad for little gifts. But never mind. God has wonderful things planned for you, I just know it. So, what do you want me to say if the subject of Simon Yoder comes up again?"

"Absolutely nothing," Anna said firmly. "It's Christmas, and I want to enjoy the season without worrying about what people are saying, especially when it's nonsense. Lizzie has a houseful, and with the new tenants moving in at the farm, it's very busy. Once Amanda Yoder's wedding is over and they've left on their wedding trip, things will settle down."

"How are Eva and Lester settling in?" Mollie wrapped both hands around her mug, as though the warmth helped with the ache, and sipped her tea.

"Very well," Anna said. "They have a lot of help. Two of Eva's brothers are here, and the elder brought his teenage sons. They came to the singing last night. The Kanagy sitting room hasn't seen such a crowd since church was there last."

"Two of her brothers?" Mollie's brown eyes lit with interest. "Priscilla didn't mention that. Which ones?"

Why hadn't she kept away from the subject of the singing? Anna thought with an internal groan. "Neil and Albert. Albert is the one with the *Kinner*. Two boys—Rafe and Elmer—and four girls, but the girls apparently stayed home with their *mamm*."

"And Neil is single still?"

"*Ja.*"

"From what I hear, he must be getting on for thirty. Way past time to be finding a wife. Maybe that's why he's here."

Oh dear, oh dear. "Look," Anna said, doing her best to sound casual, "why don't you open your present?"

"Don't you want me to wait until Christmas?" Mollie said in surprise.

"Not if you can use it sooner."

To Anna's relief, Mollie took the bait, attacking the wrappings with delight and anticipation. She lifted the lid and drew out the contents with an indrawn breath. "Oh, Anna."

Anna had made the lap quilt in Mollie's favorite colors, in the Tulips pattern. Each flower was a different spring color—yellow, lavender, peach, pink—with green leaves and stems on a soft taupe background. This past summer, Anna had quietly connived with the mothers of households with teenage girls, who wore colors she would never dare to, to collect the scraps for the quilt.

"I chose a wool batting and a flannel back, so that you'd be extra warm under it this winter."

"Ach, what a *gut* friend you are." Mollie leaned across the corner of the table to hug her. "Maybe someday I can find a way to be as good a friend to you."

"You are, every day," Anna assured her. Dear Mollie. No matter how heavy her burdens, with no family in the township now that her mother had passed on, and having to rely on the charity of the church and a small bequest from her parents since her hands were too arthritic to work, she still had the gift of gratitude and of making another feel appreciated and loved.

As Anna folded the wrapping paper and put it in the kindling box, Mollie shook out the lap quilt and laid it across her legs. "It feels like a friend's warm hand," she said. "*Denki,* Anna. You don't know what this means to me."

"Making it gave me a lot of pleasure, thinking of you all warm and toasty while the snow flies outside." She took the tea things to the sink. "I'll have these washed in a minute, and then we can have a fast game of Scrabble before I have to go home and get *Dat*'s supper."

Mollie rubbed her hands in glee. "Hurry up, then, and prepare to be beaten."

And in the fierce competition of the game, the subject of Neil Wengerd did not come up again.

By seven o'clock Sunday morning, there were nine inches of snow on the ground. Lester and *Dat* conferred and decided the two families would just walk over the creek and up the hill to Lizzie's. "I wasn't looking forward to going to all the fuss of driving such a short distance," *Dat* confided to Lester. "Too many deep ditches on this side of the township, and probably ice under that snow. Better to all walk together, if some of your young men will break the trail for us."

To Anna's relief, Neil just waved in their direction as he, his older brother, and the two boys tromped off down the slope, made sure the homemade bridge across the creek was secure, and flattened a path wide enough for two people to walk together up the other side. As she and Eva reached the top, they could see the buggies of the *Gmee* streaming in for the Christmas service. In Whinburg Township, the worship year began with the birth of Christ, and the preachers would speak from the first two chapters of either Matthew or Luke.

While the boys went to help with unhitching others' horses and taking them into Byron's spotless barn, Anna saw that on the front door, her nieces had hung a beautiful Christmas welcome in a wreath of evergreens and holly. There was none on the door of the big machine shed, of course, and inside was equally plain, with the benches set up in rows facing the chairs of the bishop, deacon, and two preachers.

Anna waited with the other single women until it was time for them to go in, following the married ladies to the women's side and taking her place in order of age between Alina Esch and the Grohl sisters, as she had since she had turned sixteen. When the single men filed in, just ahead of a gaggle of teenage boys, she absolutely refused to raise her head to see where Neil would sit. Someone observant, like Mollie Graber four rows up, could intercept such a glance and write meaning into it that wasn't there.

When the *Vorsinger* began the first hymn, she rose into the singing, making out the voice of Cora Swarey without diffi-culty, though it was clear the girl was doing her best not to stand out from the other voices. And then later, the sermon, telling the story of the very first Christmas and the birth of God's gift to the world. It was Anna's favorite story—one she could listen to over and over and always find something new to appreciate in it. This year, a faithful Father's message to her seemed to be "little miracles." A little child. Thoughtful neigh-bors. Sparrows in the trees, showing hope that there would be nests and chirping babies once winter was ended.

And a man's return, bringing her heart back to her.

Anna blinked back the tears before they betrayed her and focused on the preacher's words.

Afterward, the lunch was a simple one—sandwiches, thick slices of bread with peanut-butter marshmallow spread, *Bohnesuppe* that was so thick with beans and chunks of pork and root vegetables that it could almost be called a stew. It would really stick to the ribs for the folks with a cold drive home. Normally, people would form groups outside to digest their meal and talk over the doings of the community, fellowshipping and enjoying each other's company on this day of rest. But with the temperature hovering around freezing and the house full to bursting, it made more sense for people nearby to invite others to their homes.

Which was how Anna heard *Dat* agree with pleasure that he and Anna would like nothing better than to spend the afternoon with Eva and Lester and their visitors.

She would get through it, she told herself. Who knew how many days or weeks Neil would stay in the township? She'd already gotten through their first meeting, and a second one, too. She could do this again, and for as many times as she needed to before he went back to Colorado and set her heart free for good.

After an energizing tramp home, the boys stayed outside to build a snow fort, leaving the five adults in the sitting room with cups of coffee and plates of cookies ... and Anna realized that somehow she was going to have to make conversation.

Eva was an easy talker, always interested in one's life no matter how ordinary and narrow it might be. Lester could converse on nearly any subject, but Anna could see within minutes that farming was his love, the place he believed that

God had put him to serve the great husbandman Himself. *Dat* was always interested, too, but it was the doing of it that he found difficult. He knew all the latest farming techniques and the equipment it took to make them work, but they never seemed to work for him. Anna could only be grateful for Lester and his convictions. The farm would prosper now, and this summer the fields would wave with corn and soybeans the way they'd done in *Grossdaadi*'s time.

Neil leaned over to Anna's chair. "I wonder if you'd have a moment to show me the barn?" he said in a low tone. "Even though I work on a ranch whose principal stock is buffalo, it seems the owners are interested in buying a few head of cattle as well. Maybe we could have a look at the dairy cows?"

Anna hardly knew what to say. Their dairy cows were the same as anyone else's, and they had nowhere near as many as Byron and Lizzie, for instance. But if that was what he wanted …

"Of course," she said. "Just let me get my coat and put my boots on."

They heard the boys shouting and whooping with glee on the north side of the house, where the drifts were deeper, as they walked across the yard to the barn, their feet squeaking in the fresh snow. It had begun again, and from the looks of the clouds, would keep on right through the night.

Anna went to push open the bank barn's huge sliding door, when Neil stopped her and did it himself. Inside, the air was warm with the smell of livestock and chickens and hay and harness oil. The horses sidestepped and rolled their eyes to look at them, and when they saw it was only Anna, relaxed and went back to munching. Their few cows didn't even look up. The chickens came over to see if there were treats in her apron pockets, and disappointed, went back to hunting for spiders in the hay.

"You can't really be interested in these girls," Anna said, patting the flank of one of them with affection. "Does the ranch want exotic breeds or plain and simple Jerseys for milk?"

"A mix of both, I think," he said. "But you're right. I've already made up my mind. I just wanted an opportunity to talk without everyone in the family listening in."

He wanted to talk to her? Alone? Anna's heart gave a great bump and began to gallop.

But he seemed in no hurry to start. He leaned on the pen, his arms folded on the top rail, watching the cows ignoring them.

Anna could stand it no longer. "Do you—are you enjoying Colorado? I mean, I heard you say at the singing that you liked what you did, but a man's life is more than what he does for work, of course."

"You'd know that better than anyone."

What did he mean? Was he saying something about *Dat's* ability to farm—the reason his sister and Lester had taken over? She could see how a man with a natural affinity for farming and animals would shake his head in wonder at how anyone could be so bad at it, but she couldn't imagine Neil saying something like that to her. Not with the intent to hurt. It must be something else.

"Tell me about the church there," she said at last.

"It seems as though half our *Youngie* are here."

"Really? Are there not so many?"

"Our numbers are slowly increasing as more and more families come and settle. For the first few years, I'm told, there weren't even enough to make teams for a volleyball game."

Anna tried to imagine it. "Here, they sometimes have two and three nets going all at once, with a line waiting to take a player's place each time the ball changes sides."

"That's Lancaster County for you."

Oh, why were they talking about volleyball and not something more important? Or was their shared past so far in the dark ages that it was not even relevant, never mind important?

"How many more weddings will you have before spring?" he asked. "A dozen? More?"

"Around a dozen, I think," she said. From cows to volleyball to weddings. Was there a point to this jumping bean of a conversation? "Byron's niece, of course. Amanda and Joshua the day after tomorrow. In January, there are three in the first week alone. After that, they're more spread out. The bench wagon is getting a lot of use."

"I'm surprised that some I used to know haven't been spoken for," he said idly, still gazing at the cows. Anna's heart had calmed, but now it picked up its pace again. Was he—? Would he—? "Malinda Kanagy, for instance. She's still the prettiest girl in the township. Is it making her that picky?"

Anna felt like a cake that had been taken out of the oven and fallen flat.

"I don't know," she said hoarsely. "I imagine she is waiting to be shown God's choice, like the rest of us."

"Seems like there would be plenty of choice here," he said. "Are all the men afraid of her?"

"Why would they be afraid? She's nice, and a good cook, and she and her mother and little sister manage a huge garden and house."

"That's not what I meant." He turned toward her, leaning on one elbow. "Sometimes with just a look or a gesture, a woman can make a man feel he doesn't quite measure up. So he's afraid to ask her for a drive home or on a date. Maybe she's like that."

No. No, she could not stand here and listen to this. To know that while he may have forgiven her, he had not forgotten. Not by a long shot.

"I'm cold," she choked out before her throat closed altogether. "I'm going back to the house."

She wasn't cold. Not on the outside, at least. But on the inside, her poor flattened heart had just received such a chill that she didn't think it would ever recover.

Chapter Four

Mondays were wash day in Whinburg Township. In summer, it always gave Anna pleasure to see their clothes flying on the line, drying almost as soon as the breeze caught them. But in winter, they couldn't use the outside line or her dresses and *Dat*'s pants and shirts would freeze into planks. Instead, she hung things up on two lines in the barn loft. Which was the only reason that Anna heard the telephone ringing in her father's shop on the other side of the hedge.

By the fifth ring, she had gathered that *Dat* was not working in there. She scrambled down the ladderlike stairs and dashed the short distance across the snowy lawn to get it. *Dat* couldn't have been gone long—the workshop was warm from the potbellied stove.

"Hallo?" she answered breathlessly.

"Hallo, Anna, it's Amanda Yoder."

"Only until tomorrow," she said with a smile, trying to calm her breathing. "How does it feel?"

"As though I couldn't wait so long to take Joshua's name,"

Amanda confessed, half laughing. "I'm calling to see if you would like to come over this evening for a moonlight sleigh ride. Say about six? One or two say their fathers will hitch up their sleighs. We'll begin here with cocoa and then end up across the big field at Paul and Barbara Byler's place."

"Goodness, Amanda," Anna said in surprise. "Don't you have last-minute things to do? How can you be planning a jamboree tonight, of all nights?"

Amanda laughed. "Most of the preparations are all done. Who wants to sit in *Mamm*'s living room fretting about how slowly the time is passing? I want to be with my friends one last time before we all are with our own families for Christmas." She paused. "After the wedding, we're staying for Christmas, of course. But next week is a different story. I don't know when I'll see you all again. Please, Anna. Say you'll come."

It felt lovely to be included. "Of course I will."

"And you'll let Neil know at the big house? I've had a special request for him."

Anna went still. "Oh? From whom?"

"It's a secret," Amanda teased. "You don't mind, do you?"

Amanda meant did she mind carrying the message. Nothing more. "Not at all," Anna said. "I'll go over right now."

She hung up slowly and buttoned up her coat before stepping out of the shop. She met her father coming down the path. "*Dat*, I've just been invited to a sleigh ride tonight, so we'll eat dinner early. Is four all right?"

"Ja, whatever you like, *Dochsder*. I'll just be here, trying out a new design."

He might be a poor farmer, but his birdhouses were little works of art, and the tourists carried them away in droves in the summer. If only that had been enough to pay the mortgage every month. But those worries were behind them now. She smiled at his eagerness to get in the door and girded her loins to go home. No, to the big house. Would she ever stop thinking of it as home?

"Anna," Eva said in surprise, opening the door and stepping back to let her in. "You don't have to knock. Goodness me, I hope you think of this house as much your home as you ever did."

Which would put her right back to the kind of thinking she had to get over. "That's kind," she said. "But it's best if I don't. You might find me moved back in!"

"Once all my rapscallion menfolk go back to their own homes, I'll be wishing I had more company." Eva led the way into the kitchen, where she lifted the coffee pot with an inquiring look. When Anna nodded, she poured two cups. "But isn't that the way? So often we wish things were different, and when they are, we wish them back the old way."

Anna poured cream into her coffee and took a satisfying sip. "I haven't come for a visit, because I know you're busy with the washing. Don't forget we have the lines in the barn loft. I put our things on one, but the other is free for you."

Eva rolled her eyes. "I never knew so many pairs of pants and socks existed. How did my mother manage?"

Anna smiled. The way Amish mothers always had and always would manage. "Amanda Yoder has invited Neil to a sleigh ride tonight. I wonder if you could pass on the message? Six o'clock at the Isaac Yoders for cocoa."

"Are you going?" Eva gazed at her over the rim of her mug.

Anna nodded. "She says the work is all done, and it will be a farewell to her friends close by. We weren't in the same buddy bunch, since she's three years younger than me, but still, we

Youngie on the farms close to Willow Creek have known each other most of our lives. And of course she knew Neil when he lived here, too."

"It will be fun for all of you," Eva said, "and I'll be sure to tell my brother. Goodness, what a change this must be for him. Out there on that buffalo ranch, he says he rarely gets the chance to mix with the *Youngie* in the district." She shook her head. "How is he ever going to find a wife if he doesn't get off the ranch to go courting? I'm so glad he came to us for Christmas. I keep praying that one of the *Youngie* here will catch his eye. Like that Kanagy girl. She seems so calm and kind, for all she's so good-looking. Someone like her would be perfect for him."

Anna was not about to show what a blow to the heart those artless words were. "I'm sure a man like Neil would find a way if he wanted to." She emptied her mug. "I must go. Thank you for the coffee."

She made it back to the *Daadi Haus* without seeing anyone, and the day slipped away in chores and meal preparation. But all the while, much as she tried not to, all she could think about was Neil, maybe coming home to the township with marriage on his mind. Here, where there were girls from good, steady families. Not so fancy that they wanted the latest gadgets for their homes and worldly clothes for their wardrobes, but sensible, wholesome young women who had put their running around behind them and had already committed themselves to God by joining church.

Girls like Malinda. How would she manage on a buffalo ranch? Would getting married mean that Neil would have to leave it and find another way to make a living in a county where jobs had to be created, since they weren't very plentiful?

A horrifying thought froze her in the act of stirring the gravy.

What if he didn't plan to take a bride back to Colorado? What if they just honeymooned there, and then he returned to farm alongside Lester? There was more than enough room in the big house for two couples and for *Kinner*. What if Anna had to spend the rest of her life next door to him, watching him walk hand in hand with his bride, watching him lift his children over his head to make them laugh, watching him grow old with a woman who was not herself?

Anna smelled something scorching and hastily turned down the gas under the pan. The gravy would be too dark, but *Dat* probably wouldn't even notice.

She must not think these thoughts. Surely *der Herr* did not have such a life in mind for her. But if He did, it would take a lifetime of prayer to make her willing for it.

AT QUARTER TO SIX, all bundled up in knitted mittens and a warm woolen muffler, Anna had just closed the yard gate and was striking out across the snowy field when a shout behind her made her stop and turn.

"Anna! Wait up!" Neil, a black knit cap pulled down over his ears and his black felt hat on top of that, broke into a jog and caught up to her in seconds. "Why didn't you wait for us to go together? I'd have hitched up the buggy."

Because I can't bear to be near you and not be yours. "I like walking in the snow. With this path cleared, it's no effort. It's a beautiful night for a sleigh ride, isn't it? Look at that moon. Past the half."

"Look at that ring around it. It's going to warm up." He let her go ahead of him on the narrow path with boot prints frozen into it. "It will all be slush by the end of the week."

"But not for Christmas," she said. "No mud, no slush, no buggies stuck in the ditch on their way to Christmas dinner. Just a fairyland of white."

"Amanda's wedding might be a different matter." His boots crunched in the snow behind her, and she knew by some old instinct he was on the alert in case she slipped.

"We must leave that up to *der Herr*."

"That, and many other things."

It was the kind of obvious truth a person might say to an acquaintance. Or maybe it was a hint. "What do you mean?"

"Oh, nothing," he said. "I'm learning to wait on God's timing, out there in Colorado. But sometimes it's hard."

"It's hard for most of us, I think," she replied. What did he want so much that made it hard to wait? A wife?

"Especially for you girls, *ja?*"

"We have to wait for someone to ask us on a date," she said pertly, "but everyone has to wait on God, to know His will for our lives."

"Do *you* have to wait around for dates? Not an Esch, surely."

She couldn't remember the last time she'd been asked out. Most of her age group had married long ago, and Emma Stolzfus had married the nicer of the two widowers with children in the neighborhood. "I have better things to do than to wait around for anyone," she informed Neil airily over her shoulder. "It's you men who have to put yourselves out there and take the risks. We women simply get to choose."

"And you haven't chosen?"

She had to get him off this subject before she was completely humiliated. "Your sister believes *you're* here to find a wife." She opened the cattle gate into the Yoder field and waited for him to pass her before she closed it again.

"My sister needs to mind her own business." Was that only amusement she heard in his voice? Or was there a little annoyance that Eva couldn't keep his secret?

"Then maybe I should tell you," she said, "that Amanda had a special request for you to be invited tonight."

"A special request? From you?"

Oh, if only. But that would have taken more nerve than she possessed. "Why would I need to do that? No, it's a mystery. She wouldn't tell me." They could hear the generator running, powering the yard lights that shone down on the crowd of *Youngie*. The horses were already hitched up, the light glinting on the runners of the old-fashioned sleighs that only really came out at Christmas for frolics like this. "But I'm sure you'll find out who it is, and sooner rather than later."

"Anna, what if I—"

But she couldn't bear to listen to him speculate on who it might have been. She hurried on ahead and was engulfed in the laughing crowd of young people, all bundled up just as warmly as she was. They sipped from cups of hot cocoa that steamed in the cold air, the marshmallows bumping their noses and making the girls laugh. When it came time to load up, she made good and certain she wasn't in the same sleigh as Neil. All the same, she couldn't help but notice the way the crowd swirled and shuffled, and somehow Malinda Kanagy wound up next to him, facing forward in the family sleigh, with Priscilla Mast and Joe Byler facing them. Freddie, one of her Esch cousins, climbed up in front with Rosanne Kanagy, making more than one of his friends whistle and hoot before, red-faced, he got the horses moving.

Anna chose the open sleigh with its slatted sides and a good crowd of passengers. With Amanda beside him on its front bench, Joshua King lit the lamps and then shook the reins over the backs of the Yoder plow horses, and the sleigh jerked and set off. The runners sang in the snow, clouds of steam puffed from the horses' nostrils, the sound of their hooves muffled. Out of the yard, through the gate, and over the fallow field they went, the stars glimmering above them, and the wind of their passing whipping color into their cheeks.

"Didn't take him long to make his move," one of the young men said unhappily to the boy sitting next to Anna. He was watching the backs of Malinda's and Neil's heads in the sleigh in front of them. "You don't think she'll fall for him, do you?"

"That Colorado cowboy?" the other boy said with a snort. "Not Malinda. Not unless he owns the ranch he works on."

"He doesn't," the first one said. "Only a share. But there's no telling with girls, is there?"

"*Ja*, true," his companion said with a sigh. "Nothing but the best ain't good enough for her, you ask me."

The two familiar heads in the back of the sleigh were tipped close in conversation and laughter, and Anna had to look away, as though the people coming along behind them in the third sleigh were far more interesting.

So Neil was making his move, was he? There was no doubt in Anna's mind that the "special request" had come from Malinda. She had claimed her choice, and everyone had taken it for granted that it was her right to do so. After all, it seemed nearly every eligible boy and man in the district had courted her without success. Perhaps no one would blame her for looking farther afield.

Someone pressed a handkerchief into her mittened hand, and Anna jumped. "Looks like the wind is bothering your eyes, too," the girl on her other side said with a grin. "I already used it. You go ahead."

Anna wiped the hot tears away and did her best to school her face into anything but what she really felt.

Ahead, someone shouted, and she realized they were going down the short slope to the road bridge across the creek. The lights of the Byler place sent welcoming beams from the top of the hill farther on. But something was wrong. Anna's spine stiffened.

Joshua King called out to Freddie, "Slow down! The sleigh will get ahead of the horse! Freddie, pull up!"

But it was already too late. Freddie hauled on the reins, but he was clearly not as experienced a driver as Joshua. The horse went down on its haunches, and the sleigh swung sideways and crashed into the stone abutment that supported the bridge. The back lifted clear off the ground and with a shriek, Malinda Kanagy and Neil Wengerd were thrown out of their seats and into the rushing darkness below.

Chapter Five

Joshua King brought the horses to a clattering, sliding halt on the bridge, and he and his fiancée leapt down. While Amanda held the horses' heads and spoke quietly to them, the two boys who had been sitting next to Anna scrambled out and ran to get the downed horse out of its harness before it injured itself in its struggle.

Anna found herself out of the sleigh before she even knew she had moved, slipping and sliding down the bank after Neil and Malinda. The creek was not deep, but a thin sheet of ice had already glazed it, broken in sharp shards where the two had gone in. She met Neil sloshing to the bank with Malinda's limp body in his arms.

"I'm all right," he said hoarsely. "Landed in a snowbank. She went in the creek. *Ach, mein Gott, hilfe mich!*"

"Help!" she shouted to the ones above. "Malinda needs help!"

In moments it was clear to her that ranch work had given Neil such strength in his legs and arms that he was able to carry Malinda up the slope to the road with only one slip in the snow.

Even then, he caught himself before his limp burden could come to any harm.

"We have to be quick," he said as Anna scrambled up after him, gasping with the effort. "She's going to freeze if we don't get her indoors quickly."

"Is anything broken?" Anna said. "When she went in, did she hurt her head? Is she conscious?"

"Don't think so," he said. "This is bad."

He must care, a voice said in the back of her mind. Then she recovered herself. *Good grief, Anna. How can you think of your own pain when Malinda might die?*

"Neil," she said, gathering her wits, "lay her on the floor of the big sleigh. You get in there, too. Both of you are soaked and you'll freeze." She turned to the small crowd. "You, you, and you," she said to three of the girls. "Lie down on either side of Malinda and on top of her. We have to keep her warm until we get her to Bylers'. It's too far to take her back to the Yoder place."

Wordlessly, Neil did as he was told, and the girls scrambled up to form a kind of human quilt around and over them, wrapping their arms tightly around both Malinda and Neil to lend them their body heat. Anna heard muffled sounds of embarrassment and apology, but so far it hadn't occurred to anyone to argue with her.

"Joshua!" Anna called. "Malinda and Neil won't make it in this cold more than a few minutes. We have to get them inside at Bylers'."

For answer, he climbed up on the seat and hauled Amanda up beside him.

"Freddie." Anna shook the young man's arm, which was wrapped around Rosanne Kanagy. They stood at the back of the broken sleigh as though undecided what to do. The poor girl was in hysterics and Anna couldn't blame her—narrowly missing her elder sister's fate by who knew what narrow margin. "Freddie!"

He finally met her eyes. "I'm so sorry, Anna. I didn't mean to—I didn't know the sleigh would—"

"Freddie, there's no time. You have to call nine-one-one."

"What?" he said blankly. "I don't—"

"You do so have a cell phone, and you know I know it. Tell them to send an ambulance to Bylers'. Malinda's unconscious. She could be really hurt."

Rosanne wailed even louder.

"Freddie!" Anna shouted when he just stared at her.

"All right, all right."

"Everyone walk up the hill," she ordered. "Joshua, let's go."

While Freddie explained to the dispatcher what had happened and, for a wonder, didn't apologize twenty times in the process, Joshua got them over the bridge and up the shallow grade to the Bylers' lane. In the yard, the human quilt disentangled itself, and Neil carried Malinda into the warm house, past a white-faced Barbara Byler, who wordlessly led them back to a bedroom on the ground floor.

Anna felt like collapsing with relief that they had managed the entire rescue in less than five minutes. *Oh please, dear Lord, please be with Malinda. Please save her, if it be Your will. Make her well again. We need her.*

For the first time, she realized that the community of *Youngie* in Whinburg Township did need Malinda. Her calm kindness, her natural authority, her gentle way of making everyone comfortable were as much a part of their doings together as the hymns they sang Friday nights. Every drop of jealousy and envy that had ever curdled and soured in the bottom of Anna's heart melted away at the prospect that the young woman might not survive her ordeal. And hope and assurance in God's care for His child flowed in to replace them as, in the distance, she heard the siren.

In less than a minute, the ambulance from the county hospital pulled up in front of the house, its lights flashing in a whirl of blue and red. Two EMTs jogged into the bedroom with a backboard and a backpack of equipment, while Anna gathered herself together to give as calm an account as she could to the third EMT.

When they came out with Malinda on the stretcher, Anna could see her eyelids flutter open. Her heart leaped with hope.

"Her vitals are good, but we'll take her in," one of them told the EMT with Anna. "With a possible head injury and maybe hypothermia, better safe than sorry. These kids did well to get her someplace warm so fast."

Malinda only had time to smile weakly at Anna as they went out the door.

And Anna only had time to smile back. A real smile, full of hope and encouragement. The kind of smile a woman would give a friend.

After the ambulance had roared off down the county road, no one really felt like being festive. Instead, the Byler twins, Jake and Joe, and their father Paul went down to see if the broken sleigh could be brought up to the barn for repairs, or if it was beyond hope.

As it turned out, the runners were still attached, so one of their horses pulled it into the barn, but it wouldn't be taking anyone anywhere for a long time. Anna's eyes went wide as she saw it go past the living-room windows. The entire rear right side was stoved in where it had hit the stone bridge abutment.

Neil was given a pair of Paul's pants to go home in while Barbara dried his wet ones. The *Youngie* straggled back to the Yoder farm, where their own buggies waited. As they crested the hill, Anna could see lights in the yard of *Englisch* Henry and Sarah's home. The *Dokterfraa*, as warmly wrapped as Anna was herself, ran across to the buggy waiting in the yard, carrying a basket.

"She'll be taking cures for Malinda to the Kanagy house," Amanda said. "But she won't find anyone home. The Kanagys will have gone to the county hospital—except for Rosanne. Her *mamm* sent her home with Priscilla Mast for the night."

"What a thing to have happen when it was meant to celebrate your wedding," Anna said.

Amanda's face was pale and tight with worry. "What was I thinking?" she sighed. "This is all my fault."

Neil shook his head so decidedly that melted snow flicked off his knit cap. Goodness only knew where his hat had fallen, back there under the bridge. "It is not, Amanda. It's my fault. I should never have let Freddie drive the sleigh. It never occurred to me he hadn't taken a loaded sleigh out before—only empty. I blame myself." He began to jog down the slope toward the *Dokterfraa*.

"Where are you going?" Anna called.

"I'll see if I can go with them. Then I'll get a lift somehow to the hospital. You'll be all right for the walk home?"

"Of course, but—"

But Neil was already out of earshot, his long legs carrying him down the slope and into the yard, where after a brief exchange, he vaulted into *Englisch* Henry's buggy, and it set off down the lane at a rapid clip.

Toward the Kanagy farm. And after that, to the hospital. Where, by then, the young woman who clearly held his heart might open her eyes and see him at her bedside. He might take her hand. And without a word, everything would be settled between them.

Which was as it should be. Malinda deserved a good man like Neil, after so long a wait in obedience to the will of God. But oh …

Blinking back hot tears, Anna whispered *guder nacht* to Amanda and made her solitary way home across the snowy fields.

THE NEXT DAY, as the *Gmee* began to gather at eight in the morning in the Yoder home for Amanda and Joshua King's wedding, word quietly went around the congregation that the hospital would be keeping Malinda for one more day, releasing her on Christmas Eve. They were worried about hypothermia, but as Rosanne Kanagy had told Priscilla Mast, who told Anna, "Her father thinks the doctor is just being extra cautious. We got her into the house and warm quickly enough, and the ambulance came really fast. I'm just glad the middle of the creek hadn't iced over more with a clear night, or for sure and certain, she would have had broken bones, and the EMTs would have had their work cut out for them."

As Amanda and Joshua made their vows to each other, Anna found it necessary to look away from the bride's radiant face. But when she did, the vivid memory of the broken trail of open water where Neil had gone in to get Malinda, stunned and helpless, intruded on her thoughts. Willow Creek wasn't deep —maybe only three or four feet—but still. The *gut Gott* had surely been looking out for Malinda to place Neil exactly where he was needed. Anna had better get over her despair that he had taken that seat beside the young woman in the sleigh. Imagine if it had been someone who wasn't as strong, or as quick-thinking!

The wedding ended with a hymn, and then the bride and groom and their *Newesitzern* proceeded to the *Eck*, while the living room was swiftly transformed from a place of worship to a busy arrangement of tables and benches where the food would be laid out. Anna kept a quiet smile on her lips and her hands busy so that no one—especially Eva—would have the slightest clue that on the inside, she was a storm of worry and regret and hope that Malinda would be all right. That Neil's future wife would be all right.

The effort exhausted her. She wasn't a bit sorry to tell *Dat* she'd drive home with him instead of staying for the singing.

On Christmas Eve morning, word came like a wonderfully wrapped gift that Malinda was indeed home and able to have just a few visitors.

Just a few, as often happened in their district, turned out to be quite the crowd.

Anna hesitated between the big dining room and the living room of the Kanagy home, where Malinda lay on the sofa wrapped in one of her own Delectable Mountains quilts in shades of raspberry, black, and periwinkle blue. Her *Kapp* was crisp and freshly starched, and under it her blond hair was neatly pinned. She wore a green dress in honor of Christmas that made her skin look as fine as porcelain.

And sitting next to the sofa was Neil Wengerd, hands

clasped loosely between his knees, looking as though he would like to shoo everyone from the room so that Malinda could have a moment's peace. As it was, Simon Yoder and Jake Byler vied for the coveted chairs on her other side, by the foot of the sofa. Simon and Jake, of all the *Youngie* in the township were the least likely to catch Malinda's eye. Anna shook her head and tried not to roll her eyes. The most likely to get into a scrape, more like … the most likely to flirt for the fun of it or smoke behind the barn or get into some worldly trouble late at night.

Around the room, chairs had been dragged in. Here were Amanda's friends from Colorado, though how well they knew Malinda was a mystery. Here were Priscilla Mast and her boyfriend Joe, Jake's twin. Priscilla was helping Malinda's brother and sister with answering the door and asking if newcomers would like coffee.

"So you're safe and well," Simon was saying to the patient as Anna stood between the two rooms taking it all in. "You don't look any the worse for wear."

"What he means is that we're *glad* you're safe and well," Jake said, nudging Simon so hard in the ribs that he rocked on his chair. "Anybody heard from Freddie?"

"He came during visiting hours at the hospital last night." Malinda's voice was husky, as though she were coming down with a cold. Anna hoped not. Maybe it was something they'd done in the emergency room.

"*Ja*, I bet he did," Simon said scornfully. "He better have apologized."

"Simon," one of the young men from Colorado said in a reproving tone. "That's between him and Malinda."

"He did, about twenty times," Malinda said calmly. "So you can settle down, Simon Yoder. Anyone could have misjudged the weight of that sleigh. I know I did. And you would have, too. Don't tell me you wouldn't."

For about two seconds, Simon looked like a cockerel ready to rear up and peck. But with an effort of self-control, he settled back in his chair. "You're right. We've driven down that slope to the creek a hundred times and never thought it was all that steep." He handed her a gaily wrapped package with a sprig of holly taped to the top in lieu of a bow. "This is for you."

"Delivering a cure from your *mamm*?" Malinda slit the paper. "She brought a basket full the other night. I'm going to float away on a wave of herbal tea, though I have to say it's helping." She tilted her head toward the mug on the table by her elbow. A mug that Anna recognized as having been made by *Englisch* Henry.

"No, a cure from me," Simon said.

Malinda pulled the paper away and gazed at the box of six handmade truffles. "Why, Simon, did you have to go all the way into Whinburg this morning to find these? I'm surprised that new chocolate shop is open on Christmas Eve."

To Anna's astonishment, a slash of red burned into Simon's cheeks and just as quickly faded. "No," he said, and offered no further details. "I hope you like them."

"I'm sure I will." She smiled at him. "*Denki*. That's so kind."

"I brought something, too." Jake leaned over and set a pint jar of jam on her lap, a small paper doily wrapped over the seal and secured with a cheerful red and gold cord. "*Mamm* sends her best and hopes you get well soon."

Malinda smiled at him. "Raspberry. My favorite. Tell your *mamm denki* for her kindness—with this, and with all she did for me that night."

Anna glanced down at the quart jar of plum jelly she held. Not Malinda's favorite. Malinda must have seen the movement, for she beckoned Anna over.

Neil got up from his chair next to Malinda's mug of tea. "Anna," he said. *"Setze sich hier."*

How kind he was to offer her his seat. She gave him a brief, grateful smile before settling on the chair, still warm from his long body.

Malinda pushed herself up on the sofa cushions to see her directly. "I'm told I have you to thank that I didn't freeze to death."

Anna stared at her in astonishment. "Me? But I didn't do anything. Well, other than shout at poor Freddie to get out his cell phone and call nine-one-one."

Poor Freddie indeed. His secret was out now. The phone had probably already been confiscated by his parents, despite the fact that it might have saved a life.

Malinda shook her head. "That's not what I heard. A reliable source says you ordered some girls to make a human blanket all around me. That without it, both Neil and I would have probably had hypothermia for true, instead of its just being a little worry for the doctor."

Anna had forgotten all about that in the greater fear that they might not make it up to the Byler house in time. "Anyone would have done the same," she mumbled, her face hot.

"But anyone didn't," Malinda said gently. "You did. You took charge. Phone. Human blanket. The *gut Gott* knew what He was doing when He prompted you to join us. And I'm grateful to Him ... and to you, Anna."

The whole room was staring at her. Anna felt like sinking into the floor in embarrassment. Instead, tongue-tied, she looked away from Malinda's grateful eyes ... and straight into those of Neil Wengerd.

In the space of two seconds, she read his face, and a revelation speared through her mind to lodge right in her heart.

Neil.

Neil had gone to the hospital and found Malinda awake, just as Anna had imagined. They may have decided on their future there and then. With the way he had been occupying this chair so protectively, it certainly looked possible. But he had found time to tell Malinda what he'd seen—the small part Anna had played in her rescue. And, knowing him, he'd probably downplayed his own part in it.

He had thought well of her and hadn't been afraid to show it to another. Did that mean that after all these years, a new love had finally allowed him to forgive her?

Chapter Six

Anna was thankful to surrender her chair to one of Malinda's cousins, who had arrived with her family in an *Englisch* taxi-van from over east of Strasburg. They had come for Christmas, and with the family's arrival, many of the *Youngie* also gave up their chairs and collected coats and boots before they left.

Anna had slipped out the door and was halfway down the lane when she heard the rapid crunch of footsteps in the snow behind her. Human footsteps, not a horse. She arranged a smile on her lips and looked over her shoulder in case the person was in a hurry and wanted to go around her.

Rosanne Kanagy pulled her sweater tight across her chest. "Brr! Anna, I'm glad I caught you. My sister was supposed to give this to you, but she forgot."

Malinda had something for her? Puzzled, Anna said, "What is it?"

"Just a *Brief*. Mollie Graber was at the hospital yesterday getting some tests done, and before the *Englisch* taxi came to get her last night, she came up to visit. She asked Malinda if she would give it to you."

A letter from Mollie? Why hadn't she just mailed it? More important, why hadn't she told Anna she was going in for some tests? If she'd known, she could have gone with her for support.

More puzzled than ever, Anna took the envelope with her name scrawled across the front, and watched Rosanne pelt back up the lane, heading for the warmth of the house. Walking slowly, she moved to the edge of the lane to be out of the way of any incoming buggies, and pulled the *Brief* out of the envelope. The letter was written on lined paper, as though it had been torn out of someone's notebook, and covered in close hand-writing on both sides. As Rosanne had said, it was dated yesterday.

Dearest friend Anna,

It is very late and I am sitting in the hospital lobby waiting for the taxi to arrive. I would have put this off until a more convenient time, but God has laid an urgency on my heart that I must obey. Please forgive these scribbles—my handwriting has never been as neat as yours!

After the tests the doctor wanted, I went up to the ward to see Malinda Kanagy, but she was busy with a visitor. Neil Wengerd. If he had come out of more than friendship, I didn't want to disturb them, so I waited outside her room. I didn't mean to listen, but you know how voices travel. Anna, I have to tell you that, in all that time, I don't think there was a sentence without your name in it. And I remembered a few things some little birds have told me over the years I've lived here. He may have pulled that poor girl out of the creek, but from what I heard last night as they talked, it was your quick thinking that got Freddie to call 9-1-1 so that the ambulance came, and to make sure they were both warm until they got to Bylers' house.

I could say she was lucky, but I know firsthand it's not luck to have such friends as you. God's hand was in it.

When Neil left, I don't think he even saw me waiting in the corridor. Whatever you think of him, Anna, however long it has been, please forgive me for telling you that for him, I don't think it's over. He did not talk to the prettiest girl in the township like a man who's come a-courting. He talked to her about you.

He also told her he plans to leave for Colorado right after Christmas, on Saturday.

Whatever you choose to do, I hope you will forgive me for sticking my nose in. I do it out of friendship, not to be a tattle-tale. I hope you will come to see me soon. I am enjoying my beautiful lap quilt very much and think of you every time I use it. Like our friendship, it comforts me and makes me happy.

Your sister in Christ,
Mollie

Anna looked up from the letter to find herself standing in the mouth of her own lane with no memory of how she'd gotten there. Everything was the same. The mailbox with its cap of snow. The sky so clear a blue above the white fields that it nearly hurt to look at them both together. The sparrows darting in the branches of the bare maple in front of the house.

And yet ... everything was utterly changed.

For him, I don't think it's over.

Could she bear the breathless, disbelieving happiness leaping up in her heart? And then the plunge of despair. Two days. He was leaving again in two days.

She had to do something besides stand here in the snow.

Did she dare trust Mollie's instincts? Never mind that, did she dare trust her own? That lift of her heart when Neil had offered her his chair ... the peace she'd felt when he'd backed her up the night of the sleigh ride, as though he had no doubt in her ability to choose the right thing. And in the barn, when he had been talking about Malinda's prospects? Anna drew a long breath. He'd said, *I'm surprised that some I used to know haven't been spoken for.*

He hadn't been talking about the other girl at all, though the conversation had turned in that direction. He'd been talking about her, Anna.

She had two days before he left, two days in which to seize this chance God had given her. God had prompted her dear friend to show her the truth, so that the scales would fall from her eyes. So that she would see past her own mistakes and regret to what He in His goodness had planned for her if she would only reach out and take it.

Anna reached out toward the clear blue sky, the letter trembling in her mittened hand as if to show God she'd received the message. It was time to let Him make a miracle.

DAT HAD INVITED Eva and Lester and their visitors for Christmas Eve dinner at four o'clock. Tomorrow, he and Anna would be expected at Lizzie's, and Eva and Lester would be on the other side of the township at her eldest brother's. Anna and Eva had collaborated on a ham dinner with all the trimmings—mashed potatoes, string beans with a crunchy cheese topping, chicken and squash casserole, creamed corn, rolls, and three different kinds of pickles. For dessert Anna had used Mollie Graber's recipe for pumpkin pecan pie, and young Rafe and Elmer did it full justice. Neil had savored his piece of pie but had not gone for seconds. She couldn't blame him. She herself was so full that going for a walk, even at a balmy thirty-five degrees outside, seemed like a wonderful idea.

She had seen to it that Mollie came to dinner, too, and had arranged for the *Englisch* taxi to pick her up. The chatter and laughter around the table was even sweeter for her friend's being able to share it with them. After dinner, Anna would make good and sure that a nice box of leftovers went home with Mollie, enough to make lunches and dinners for three days at least.

But other than one expressive look at Anna as Neil had helped Mollie to her seat at the dinner table, her friend did not mention the contents of her letter, not even after supper, when the men had gone into the sitting room moaning about how full their stomachs were as Eva and Anna did the dishes.

When Mollie seemed to flag around eight o'clock, Anna was the first to see it. "I'll call the taxi-van," she told her. "You look tired, and I don't want you to overdo."

"Denki." Mollie sighed. "That was the best meal I've had in months. But the sauce made it *wunderbaar.*"

"The sauce?" Anna ran back over the menu in her memory. "I don't remember any—"

"Love," Mollie said with a smile. "We could have had boiled eggs, but with that sauce it would still have been the best meal ever."

Anna laughed, which made Neil look up, which made her smile take on the warmth of true happiness. He was here, in their house. And that made this Christmas unlike any other.

He blinked and, for a moment, looked as though someone had shined a big box flashlight right in his eyes.

As she was putting on her coat to go out to the shop to call the taxi, he came into the kitchen. "Anna, don't go to the expense of a taxi. You and I can take Mollie home in the buggy. It won't take me a minute to harness Jubilee."

You and I? Had any three words ever sounded so lovely? "You—but—your family—" Anna stammered.

"My family can do without me for an hour. After that meal, a little exercise is just the thing I need. Give me ten minutes."

The old Anna would have declined and found some work to do that would take her out of temptation. The new Anna shot a look at Mollie, who said not one word. But in her friend's eyes was a whole letter. A letter that Anna could read just as plainly as the one written on paper. *I told you so. It's a two-mile return trip, just the two of you—don't waste it.*

When they heard the jingle of Jubilee's harness outside, Anna saw Mollie safely settled in the front seat. She climbed into the back of the buggy, pulling the wool blanket across her knees. While Mollie chatted away to Neil, making him laugh, Anna dreamily watched the way the light of the three-quarter moon caught the planes of his cheek, giving his profile a beautifully cut clarity. He had changed out there in Colorado. Become more honed. More his own essence. She reveled in the luxury of being able to drink him in with nobody to see and make comments about it—until he turned and caught her in the act.

"All right back there?"

"Ja," she said, blushing furiously and thankful the glow of the buggy lamps didn't reach this far. "Mollie's house is the next

one, with the picket fence. She's in the basement suite. The door is around back."

Mollie clung to his arm on the snowy walk while Anna carried her walker, then after Mollie had opened the door, she gave Anna a hug on the doorstep. *"Denki,* my friends," she said. "A merry Christmas and a happy trip home. Good days to you, Neil."

"And to you," he said. *"Guder nacht."*

Mollie took the walker with another look at Anna that spoke volumes, and the door closed on her smile.

Neil offered Anna his arm. "I don't want you to slip. Looks like there's a little ice yet."

It was as though the years had never been, as they fell into step together. No tripping or awkward bumping of elbows, no jostling from one side to the other. Anna could have walked all the way back to the farm with him, but all too soon she was climbing into the front of the buggy and he was flapping the reins over Jubilee's sturdy back.

"Anna—"

"Neil—" She smiled and ducked her head. "You first."

"It was silly anyway." His gaze was on the road ahead, his voice gruff. "Just that it seems like old times."

"Yes. But I guess you probably won't be racing Jubilee like old times."

"Jubilee is not a racing horse. Not like Star." He grinned with the memory. "What a beauty she was."

"And how she terrified me."

He glanced at her. "You're not so easily frightened these days, if the other night is anything to go by."

"Not in some ways. Growing up and learning what you're

capable of changes things. But in other ways ...” Her voice trailed off.

“What frightens you now?” he asked. “If you don’t mind me asking.”

She took it at a canter. “You going away. On Saturday.”

“You heard.” But he didn’t react to her forwardness. What was going on in his mind? She had to know now. At once, before she burst.

“I did. But Neil, why so soon? Why not stay until the New Year? Do the buffalo need you that urgently?”

“The buffalo don’t need anyone.”

“Then why come all this way just to leave so soon?”

She thought her pounding heart might stop in the five seconds that he hesitated. Then he said, “I came back to see if ... things had changed.”

“A lot of things haven’t. But some things have.”

“Like what?”

Here was her moment. Nothing but complete honesty and *uffgeva*—the giving up of her own will—would do. The rest of her life depended on it.

“What hasn’t changed are my feelings for you,” she said baldly while *Mamm* probably spun in her grave at her forwardness. “What has changed is that now I’m willing to say so.”

Another five seconds in which she thought she might die— or grab him and shake some words out of him.

“Your feelings for me were pretty clear back then,” he said slowly. “I remember you saying that you couldn’t marry a man who couldn’t provide. You can’t imagine how much that hurt, Anna. Not that you didn’t love me. Not that your parents had said no. But that I couldn’t provide.”

“I was wrong,” she confessed. “And frightened and stupid.

Oh, Neil ... *Mamm* had just found out she had the cancer, and she didn't want the *Gmee* to know. She couldn't bear them doing for her—serving her. *Dat* was falling apart, and I was so *verhuddelt* that instead of breaking my promise to her and telling you the truth, I blurted out the first thing that came into my head." She leaned over to rest her forehead on his wool sleeve. "Of course you can provide for any woman. God has given you strength and determination and talent. I am sorry I ever said that to you."

"Your mother? Anna, I had no idea. So that was why—"

"Yes, it was quick. Only a couple of months later, God saw fit to take her home. She was in stage four before she even told us." She took a deep, shuddering breath. "By which time, you were long gone, and it was far too late to explain."

"If not for your promise, would you have married me?"

"*Dat* would still have been a mess and needed me, but *ja*," she said softly, "I would have married you."

"And he still needs you."

"Not in the same way." Jubilee took the corner to the farm, sensing his warm barn was just ahead. Anna had only minutes now. "He likes you, no matter what he might have thought about your prospects back then."

"*Ja*, I saw that at dinner. He really liked the buffalo story."

"He reads those western novels out in the shop while he waits for varnish to dry. I think in his deepest heart he'd like to ride and rope, too. But my brother-in-law Byron would have a fit if he tried it on one of the dairy cows."

Neil laughed. "I can teach him how to do it. All he needs is a bale of hay."

Anna took heart. "Does that mean you might stay a little longer?"

Jubilee turned into their lane and, when the reins went slack on his back, came to an obedient stop in the filigree shadows cast by the maple. The rising moon was caught in the branches.

"If I did, it wouldn't be for your father, or my sister, or anyone but you. Because you wanted me to."

Her heart was beating so fast, she almost couldn't speak. "I do want you to. For Christmas, and for New Year's, and for all the rest of my life."

His eyes sparkled in the light of the buggy lamps. "Are you proposing to me, Anna Esch?"

"If that's what it takes," she managed past the lump in her throat.

"You have changed. No longer afraid." Reins in his right hand, he took her hand in his left, and her breath rushed out as their fingers entwined. "Well, I've changed, too. I guess it took as much courage for you to say that just now as it did for me to come back and see if you would."

"Is that why you came back?" she whispered. "To see me?"

"Of course, *Liewi*," he said. "I didn't know what I would find, but Malinda did me a favor that night I went to the hospital, talking about everyone in the community. I realized that you'd had your chances and turned them down—chances with good providers and good church members. In my mind, there could only be one reason for that."

"There was," she said. "God showed me His choice of partner, and I didn't have the courage. Eight years of pain and endurance have been my reward for ignoring His will and my own feelings."

"I have felt the same," he confessed. "So, Anna, I accept your proposal."

"You do?" she blurted. "Even after the way I hurt you—and hurt myself?"

"*Ja*. Even after that." He leaned his forehead on hers, the way they used to do, and looked deep into her eyes. "I don't want the next eight years to be like that. Marry me, and we'll step out on God's promises together."

"Yes," she breathed. "Oh, yes."

And when he kissed her the way she'd been waiting to be kissed for eight lonely years, Anna's heart lifted up in joy. For God had been true to his promise ... and given them both a Christmas miracle.

Chapter Seven

Dearest Mollie,

Since your letter changed my life, I thought I would return the favor and send you one that I hope will bring you joy.

On Christmas Eve, Neil and I proposed to each other, and we each accepted!

I know you are laughing already because you saw this coming a mile away, but I wanted you to be among the first to know. We managed to keep our secret through Christmas Day, but when Neil didn't leave this morning as planned, the cat was out of the bag. We will have it announced in church next Sunday and then be married as soon as it can be arranged. I have been waiting eight years for this, so I'm not about to waste any more time!

We need to decide where we are going to live. I think I can make a perfectly nice home out of a Colorado bunkhouse, but Neil doesn't agree. Either we build a house for ourselves out in the Wet Mountain Valley, or he moves home to Whinburg Township. Eva and Lester have already offered him a partnership in the farm leases, and goodness knows there is enough room in the big house *for two couples and a family, if God wills it, but it is early days yet. We have time to decide.*

I think I would like a look at those buffalo, though, and I think Dat might enjoy a trip out to Colorado in the summer to see them, too. Some of the Youngie from the township who have work on the ranches could go with him so he doesn't get lost changing trains. But that is in the future.

For now, I am the happiest woman in Pennsylvania, and I look forward to a lifetime of making Neil just as happy. He says that now we are together, all that's left to want in the world is a regular supply of pumpkin pecan pie, so thank you very much for that recipe!

Your sister in His love,

Anna

THE END

I hope you enjoyed reading *The Heart's Return,* part of the Whinburg Township Amish series, and catching up with friends from my fictional township in the very real Lancaster County, Pennsylvania.

You might leave a review on your favorite retailer's site and tell others about my books. And you can find print and digital editions of my series online. I invite you to visit my website at www.adinasenft.com, or my store at moonshellbooks.com, where you can subscribe to my newsletter and be the first to know of new releases and special promotions.

Looking for more of my Amish fiction? If you haven't yet visited Whinburg Township, turn the page to read the first chapter of book one, *The Wounded Heart.* Or let your imagination travel to northwestern Montana with *The Amish Cowboy,* book one in the Amish Cowboys of Montana series!

Denki!

Adina

Excerpt

THE WOUNDED HEART © ADINA SENFT

*But do thou for me, O God the Lord, for thy name's sake:
because thy mercy is good, deliver thou me. For I am poor
and needy, and my heart is wounded within me.*
—Psalm 109:21–22 (KJV)

Chapter One

Every piece of fabric held a memory.

Amelia Beiler paused in her sorting of scraps to finger a piece of purple cotton. Sometime last spring in a moment of resolution, she'd cut it up into squares, but she knew every mark. This piece had lain under Enoch's suspenders—the cotton was worn down to the weft threads and half the dye had rubbed away. It had been his favorite shirt—the one she'd made for him in the weeks before their wedding ten years ago. The collar had never sat properly around his neck, so he couldn't wear it to church, and the side seams had a maddening way of twisting to his left. But every time he put it on he'd kissed her and said, "You've wrapped me in love, *Liewi*," and worn it to work in the pallet shop.

She'd learned a thing or two about sewing since then. And about love.

Her lips wobbled and, swallowing hard, she set the scrap aside. It was really only good for the rag bag. But maybe she'd make a quilt just for herself out of such pieces. After all, the things in the rag bag tended to be what you loved the most and wore out, didn't they? Then she could be wrapped in love, too.

It had been eleven months since the buggy accident had taken him away, but the tears still lived close to the surface where the silliest things would make them well up. The song of the wrens in the trees that woke them on summer mornings. The way his drinking glass still sat next to the kitchen sink, unused, because she always used the glass in the bathroom. His straw hat on the spindle of the rocking chair, as though he'd just hung it there. The wrens still sang and woke her up, and the boys used the glass and the hat, but the fact that Enoch was missing from all of them was enough to make the mourning begin all over again.

Genunk.

She could stand here feeling sorry for herself all day, or she could get all these scraps and squares into her basket and get over to Carrie's. Because it was Tuesday afternoon, and she, Emma, and Carrie would have two blessed hours all to themselves to plan the next quilt. The boys were in school, the pallet shop would run itself without her—she always left David in charge on Tuesdays, never Aaron—and Emma's sister-in-law was probably already at the *Daadi Haus* to spell Emma and give her a bit of a rest from caring for her parents.

Two hours. In that amount of time, you could plan a

square, visit and catch up, and remind yourself that you were a woman with a soul that needed feeding.

Amelia laced up her sturdy oxfords—no sneakers on this blustery day on the bare end of October—and wrapped her knitted shawl over her chest, tucking the ends into her black belt apron. She checked that her hair was tucked neatly into her *Kapp* by habit and that its three straight pins—one on the top and one on each side—were in order by feel. A pan of cinnamon buns and two jars of applesauce went into her carry basket, wrapped in plastic and towels. Then she left the house and let herself out the back gate into the fallow field that separated the last of the five- and ten-acre places on the edge of town from the big farms that spread themselves along Edgeware Road.

The air smelled of wood smoke and crab apples, spiced with the tang of frost. Amelia breathed deeply and set her thoughts on Carrie and Emma and their two hours. If they saw her tear up, they got distressed and fussed with cups of coffee and worried voices. That wasn't what she wanted for their time together. It was sacred to everything light and good, and she wouldn't bring a rain shower in with her if she could possibly help it.

Enoch would understand. He had loved a good laugh and the small moments that God gave a person to appreciate His gifts.

Five minutes' fast walk across the field and a hop across the creek that formed the east boundary of the Stolzfus farm brought her within sight of Emma, who waved from the front porch of the sturdy little *Daadi Haus* as if she were on a train leaving for Philadelphia. She disappeared inside and a moment later ran out the back as Amelia passed the big farmhouse where

Emma's sister Karen lived with her husband, John, and their young family. Like Amelia, Emma had a shawl wrapped tightly around her and a big bag suspiciously weighted at the bottom with the rounded shapes of canning jars.

"Hallo," she said as she joined Amelia. "Do you have all your squares ready? I tell you, I've been looking forward to this for days. Our quilting frolics are the only good thing about this time of year."

Amelia opened the access gate between the Stolzfus place and Moses Yoder's pasture and closed it behind the two of them so they wouldn't accidentally let his cows out. "The only good thing? I'd think that finishing up a winter's worth of canned fruit, pickles, and vegetables would be a wonderful *gut* thing. It took me twice as long this year because of having to run the pallet shop. I had to get the boys to help me wash jars and cut beets and apples—otherwise I'd be standing in front of that stove yet."

"All right, two good things."

"And what's wrong with fall? It's my favorite season, with all the colors and things slowing down a bit. Well, except for the —" She stopped. "Oh."

"*Ja.*" Emma kicked a stone out of their path. "Wedding season."

The remains of the Yoder cornfield brushed at Amelia's ankles, sad and brown. "You shouldn't let it bother you, dear."

Emma hauled the strap of her tote bag up onto her shoulder. "That's like telling our creek it shouldn't run downhill. I am what I am, and I get tired of hearing about it, is all."

"You make it sound like you're some kind of strange creature with five legs. There are worse things than staying *leddich.*" Like being a husbandless mother with two energetic boys and a business to run. Mothering wasn't the problem—she loved her boys and loved making a home for them. The problem was having to do a man's work on top of it—work for which she had little training and less talent.

"You haven't had Bishop Daniel introduce you as 'the senior single' lately, then, or you wouldn't say so."

Amelia squelched the urge to giggle. She would never hurt Emma by so much as a smile, but—*senior single*? Daniel Lapp had a gift for saying exactly the wrong thing. This wasn't the first time she'd wondered if, by letting the lot fall where it had, the Lord was testing him ... or the rest of the church.

"You're right," she said at last. "That would be a trial. What did you do?"

"What could I do but smile and hope the woman won't remember me?"

"You might want her to remember you if she has a brother or son in his thirties, with a nice farm."

"Any man in his thirties with a nice farm was snapped up long ago by some *schee Meedel* a foot shorter and fifty pounds lighter than me." Emma walked faster, her eyes on the ground.

"Looks don't matter, and you know it," Amelia reminded her. "The Lord gives everyone different gifts. Yours are a loving spirit and giving hands—and a brain that puts mine to shame."

Emma slowed down enough to slip an arm around Amelia's shoulders in an awkward hug as they crossed the county road and climbed the last slope. They could just see the green roof of the Miller farmhouse through bare branches.

If only there were a way to make Emma see that neither her looks nor anything else about her had to do with her being single at twenty-nine. She was warm, funny, and brave. Amelia could no more write articles for *Family Life* or *Die Botschaft* than sprout wings and fly like a barn swallow, yet Emma picked up her pen and did it. The fact that she signed them "E.S." didn't detract from the nerve it took to speak out on everything from the best way to keep cucumber pickles crisp to why dingle-dangles shouldn't be allowed to hang across the storm fronts of the young men's buggies.

Carrie must have been watching from the window, because she stepped out onto the porch as they walked into the yard, her face glowing with as much happiness as if she hadn't just seen them at church at Moses Yoder's place two days ago. *"Willkumm!"* she called. "I've been waiting for hours, you two."

"So have we." Amelia climbed the steps and hugged her. "There's a lot of hours in a whole summer."

"Come in, come in." Carrie showed them into the front room, where she would set up the quilt frame when they had the top pieced. "Help me move the dining table closer to the window. The sun comes in further now than it does in June."

"Isn't Melvin here?" Emma picked up one end and Amelia and Carrie took a corner each.

"No. He had to go to Harrisburg to see about winter work, now that the harvest is in." She looked away.

Amelia and Emma exchanged a glance and said nothing. No one ever admitted out loud that Melvin's talents did not include farming. Some men, as Amelia's *Daed* said, were born with dirt under their fingernails. And some, like Melvin, just weren't. Enoch used to casually happen upon Melvin in his fields and offer a helping hand, especially during spring, when equipment inevitably would break down because he'd forgotten to fix it during the winter, or the seed he'd laid in would be moldy, or the horses would get sick and the vet would have to be called out at huge expense.

As a result, he and Carrie were perpetually in debt, and in the slow months he had to go out among the *Englisch* to find work. Sometimes it would take him from home for a week. Once it had even been a month, when he'd taken the train to his cousin's away out there in Shipshewana to work at the RV factory installing upholstery. Amelia wondered how Carrie could bear sleeping alone in the house—why she didn't have one or two of her sisters come and stay with her when Melvin was gone. At least Amelia had the boys to give her home that lived-in feeling. Otherwise the rooms would echo with Enoch's absence and reduce her to hiding under a quilt in his reading chair, rocking and rocking as she prayed for strength.

Carrie adjusted the hand-me-down table until it lay in a square of sunlight, then clasped her hands with sheer pleasure, like a girl. "There. Now we can get started." One thing about Carrie—she might not have much, but at least she had the gift of joy. Their fields might be seas of mud, her washing machine on the fritz, and her cupboards bare of nearly everything for *Kaffi* save what Amelia and Emma had brought, but her happiness at their mere presence was enough to fill the room.

"So," Emma said, laying out two-and-a-half-inch squares in neat stacks, ordered by color, "have we decided on the piecing? Should we do a twenty-five-square Irish Chain again, like last year? That one was fun."

Amelia pulled out the pile of squares she'd been cutting and hoarding all year and reached over to put them next to Emma's. Without warning, her hand went numb and she dropped the whole thing, squares fluttering to the floor like a drift of leaves after a blast of wind.

She made a rude noise with her tongue and rubbed the circulation back into her wrist. Then she bent to gather the fabric. "Do we have enough shades of lights and darks?" she said from under the table. "We could do a Crosses and Losses, with wide borders. I'd like to try that new style of feathers, where they have them winding around a column in the middle. It's so pretty."

She surfaced to see Carrie looking a little doubtful. "It wouldn't be too *grossmeenich* of us to do that, would it? I wouldn't want anyone saying we were showing off."

"It's not like we're entering it in the county fair to try to win a ribbon," Amelia pointed out. "That *would* be showing off. This is just for us." She lifted her eyebrows, just a fraction.

Carrie said hastily, "Of course. Or maybe we could send it in to the quilt auction in Strasburg next September when they do the big fund-raiser. I like Crosses and Losses. It reminds me of flocks of butterflies."

Emma nodded, unaware that Amelia had nearly given the game away. What Emma didn't know was that she and Carrie had decided on Sunday after church that this winter's quilt would be a wedding present for Emma, should that happy day ever come. Quilting the beautiful feathered borders in the new style would be the perfect way to celebrate the beauty of their friendship as well as whatever skill God had put in the fingers of the three of them. Emma would take their friendship into her new life, covering her when times got hard and nights were cold.

Now if only the good *Gott* would put His infinite mind to providing her with a husband.

While Emma and Carrie nattered about whether the bigger pieces should be darker and the small triangles made of multi-colored scraps, or the other way around, Amelia rubbed her hand. Had she pinched a nerve somehow with all that canning? Her middle and fourth fingers were still prickling as if they had pins and needles, but at least now they would bend.

Maybe she should check with Mamm about a remedy for circulation. She'd better do it in the evening, though, and take the boys with her. If she went over on a morning, Mamm would be so delighted that she was actually consulting her about something, she was likely to keep her there all day.

By the end of the first hour, they'd managed to come to some decisions. "I like a quilt that means something," Emma said firmly. "The quilt should say something about the crosses with its lights and darks."

Since it was to be her quilt, Carrie and Amelia nodded. "There are so many choices, though," Carrie said. "What can we say with the colors we have?"

Did *Englisch* women think about these things when they pieced their quilts? Surely they must. The messages in the patterns were half the fun, even if the recipient never knew. The quilter kept her counsel and let her fabric speak for her. Tradition said, for instance, that the center square in a Log Cabin should be red, to signify the fire in the cabin's hearth. With a Sunshine and Shadow, you started with light colors in the middle, to signify the light of God in the center of life. And the—

Fire. Light. Wait. "*Meine Freundin*, what if we ... hmm..."

Carrie grinned at Emma. "Uh-oh. Amelia's had a brain wave."

Amelia began to lay out squares on the table, folding most of them in half to model the triangles of the pattern. Her heart picked up its pace, like a horse sensing that it was close to home. "What if we shaded the colors from bottom to top? Look." The quilt block grew, and she began another. "In each block we can shade the colors from dark to light, which would shade each row from dark to light. The whole pattern would look like a gradual sunrise, you see?"

Emma snatched up the colorful pile of squares. "You mean like this?"

Amelia could hardly contain herself as Emma's quick eye took in the lay of her squares and triangles and began duplicating it from the other side of the table. This was the part of quilting she loved most—the creation of patterns, the realizing of order from the chaos of bits of memory, all coalescing into a single object of beauty that spoke louder than its individual parts. Something that was utterly practical and yet as unique and lovely as the women who created it.

Carrie fetched a piece of paper and a pencil and sketched the layout as it formed. One time they'd made a new design and tried to rely on memory as they pieced it. That hadn't turned out so well—especially when Amelia brought in her squares and discovered she'd put the whole thing together backward. After that, Carrie usually made a sketch to guide them later, when the thrill of the initial creation had worn off.

"There." Carrie ran a critical eye between sketch and table, then handed the paper to Amelia. "Why don't I make coffee while you look this over? Then if you want to change anything, you can."

Emma got up and rooted in her bag and Amelia's basket, unobtrusively putting jars on the counter as if she meant to open every one and serve up a feast. Then, in the fuss of leaving, she would accidentally on purpose forget to put them back in, and Carrie would have some beautiful golden peaches to offer her husband when he came home from Harrisburg. By the time the coffee had perked and Carrie had served the cinnamon rolls, applesauce, and Emma's chocolate whoopie pies, Amelia had made a few tiny changes to the design and added its borders.

"This will be a good one," she said, tucking it into her basket. "The whole quilt will show the sunrise of our hope in the cross, won't it?" She caught Carrie's eye, and she nodded in satisfaction at a good afternoon's work. "I'll draw copies and get them to you after the Council Meeting on Sunday. Oh, speaking of patterns, I got a circle letter from Katie Yoder up in Lebanon."

"And how is she?" Emma wanted to know. "Does she have any news for us? She said in her last that she was making a baby quilt. If that wasn't a hint, I don't know what would be."

Amelia pulled the bundle of letters from all the girls in their old buddy bunch who were avid quilters. At this time of year, the circle letters went around at twice their usual speed as the women shared what they were working on or traded patterns. "You can read it. I brought them to save a stamp. Mine's already in there."

Emma retrieved Katie's letter and read it in less than a minute. Amelia didn't see how she could do that. It took her nearly a week to read a packet of letters. When Emma got them, she probably read every one of them, wrote hers, and sent the packet on, all in the same day.

"I knew it!" Emma exclaimed. "She had a boy. I hope she went with green borders instead of yellow." She looked up at a sound like the mew of a newborn kitten. "Carrie? Are you all right?"

"I'd be happy with any kind of border," Carrie said quietly. Her cheeks had gone bright red, which made her blond hair look even paler. She blinked, the long lashes that Amelia had often envied becoming slightly wet and spiky with tears.

Emma looked as though she wanted to slap herself. "Oh, dear heart, I'm so sorry. I'm a thoughtless idiot. Of all things to bring up. I didn't mean to hurt you, honest I didn't." She reached across and covered Carrie's hand with her own.

Carrie turned her palm over and returned the squeeze. "I know," she whispered. "Most of the time, I have enough to do that I don't think about it. But when Melvin is gone and it's so silent in the house..." She took a deep breath and let it out with only a little bit of a hitch. "That's when it gets to me. At least if I had babies, they'd keep me busy. I'd even welcome crying and fussing, because then I couldn't hear the silence."

"Don't be too quick to wish for that," Amelia said wryly. But deep inside, Carrie's words lodged in her heart. Hadn't she just been thinking that very thing?

"But I do. A crying baby would give me someone to hold, you see."

Amelia swallowed. "Babies take clothes and diapers and immunizations. Maybe it's God's will to keep that blessing to Himself for now, until you and Melvin can afford it."

Carrie bent her head as though there were something fascinating in her coffee cup, and nodded. No one said it, but Amelia knew perfectly well Carrie would give up what little she had if she could only have a baby. When a woman was twenty-eight and had been married for ten years, the fact that babies didn't come only looked stranger with every passing month.

"My mother-in-law was here yesterday," Carrie said in a tone so low that Amelia was glad for the silence in the house—otherwise she would not have heard her.

"All that way and back in one day?" Emma asked in amazement. "Doesn't she live in Intercourse?"

Carrie nodded. "She didn't go back. She's visiting the Daniel Lapps. Mary Lapp is her sister, you know."

"Right. And Mandy's getting married next week. The first Tuesday in November." Emma sounded perfectly calm. You'd never know what it cost her to say it—seeing that Mandy Lapp was barely nineteen.

"Did you have a nice visit?" Amelia didn't know Aleta Miller very well, except to nod hello to in church when she came down. "I imagine she's coming to help with the wedding."

"She wasn't here about the wedding," Carrie said. "Or not entirely. She had time for a ... very personal visit."

"How personal, exactly?" Amelia said slowly. This didn't sound good.

"She wanted to know if ... if everything was all right between Melvin and me. If we were ... having marital ... relations."

The clock in the kitchen ticked five times while Emma and Amelia tried to think of something more helpful to say than, *That nosy old biddy—what business is it of hers?*

"What did you say?" Amelia finally managed. She could sort of understand one's own mother asking such a question. Hers had had plenty to say about Matthew's leisurely arrival—as though a two-year wait to see a grandchild was more than a woman should have to endure. But to have your mother-in-law, whom you saw only a handful of times a year, come from twenty miles away to ask such a thing?

When Carrie looked up, the tears had dried, leaving tracks on her cheeks. "I'll have to write her a letter asking forgiveness."

"Oh, my," Emma said. "As bad as that?"

Carrie nodded. "You know how you take it and smile and take some more?" Emma shifted in her ladder-back chair, but Carrie went on without pausing, as if she'd waited so long for this chance to talk that she couldn't wait another moment to get it out. "You walk past your *Mamm*'s buddies and they put their heads together when you're out of earshot, and you just ignore it? Well, by the time Aleta got to our door, I was about full up, and when she opened her mouth and said it straight out, not even trying to put it gently or work around to the subject over coffee, it all came pouring out of me. Like she'd lanced a big, ugly boil and neither of us had a bandage ready."

Amelia could count on the fingers of one hand the number of times she'd seen Carrie angry. Aleta must have hurt her deeply to put this white, strained expression on her pretty face.

"I guess she won't be staying here while she's helping with the wedding, then?"

"Melvin would never understand if she didn't. Which is why I have to write this afternoon, or hitch up the buggy and go over there to invite her back. Not only that, I wouldn't be at peace in Council Meeting on Sunday. You know they're going to talk about forgiveness."

At least she would have peaches to eat with her humble pie tonight. Poor Carrie.

"She wouldn't tell Melvin what you said to each other, would she?"

"I hope not. I have to smooth it over before he comes home Friday. If she's here and still offended at me, then I'll have to tell him what I said to cause it. And I just can't bring myself to do that. He loves his mother, and it would hurt him to know I spoke to her that way."

"*She* spoke to *you* that way," Emma pointed out.

"I know, but I shouldn't have given it back. Most of the time we get on fairly well, but children are a sore spot with both of us."

"Doesn't Melvin have brothers and sisters with lots of babies for her?"

Melvin and Carrie had met at a band hop when they were both on *Rumspringe*, when kids came from as far as fifty miles away to dance and drink and watch each other do what was forbidden at home. It wasn't as though he'd grown up in Whinburg and they'd known his family all their lives. He'd moved here and bought this farm so Carrie would be close to her family. Melvin probably thought he was making a sacrifice for the woman he loved, but in Amelia's mind God knew what He was doing separating Carrie from her mother-in-law.

Except there were separations of distance and separations of emotion. If Carrie didn't close the gap in the latter, it would widen until she'd need more than a trip of twenty miles to heal it. And then how would she be able to take part in Communion next month with a good conscience?

"He does—four brothers and two sisters, and all but the youngest boy are married and having families." Carrie reached over to collect Amelia's empty dessert plate. "That's why I don't understand why she cares so much."

"Maybe he's her favorite," Emma suggested. "My sister Karen is Pap's favorite, and all of us know it."

"I wish Karen would come visit your folks more often." Carrie changed the subject so smoothly and sympathetically that Amelia almost missed it. "She's only on the other side of the lane. It would give you a break."

"I do, too," Emma admitted, making the conversational sacrifice for Carrie. It was clear the latter didn't want to talk anymore about her differences with Aleta, and if that meant that Emma now had to bear the burden of talking about what hurt her, she would do it. "But you know ... she's busy with her own family and running our place."

"What about Katherine? She could come for a week and let you get away," Carrie said. "She only has the three girls, and the oldest must be ten. Old enough to help with her grandmother."

Amelia buttoned her lip. Only a childless woman would think that three kids under ten would be any help at all in the sickroom after the first hour's novelty had worn off. Not that Emma's father was in a sickroom. But if he got much further than the barn, he would forget where he was and Emma and her mother would have to go out looking along the roads to fetch him back.

"Mamm would love to see them," Emma went on calmly, "but it's not so easy to get away, I guess."

Carrie was a born organizer, especially when she was organizing other people. "But if each family came for a week out of a month, or took your parents into their homes for a month at a time, you'd have only a few months when you were left to do it completely alone."

Emma shook her head and put a kettle of water on to boil for the dishes. "It wouldn't be fair to Mamm and Pap to be ferried all around the country. Pap has a hard enough time remembering where he is on a place he's lived all his life. How would he manage over in Strasburg with Katherine, or way out in New Hope with Jonas? He'd be upset every minute, and he'd set off down the road to come home not even knowing what direction he was going. It would just be too hard."

"Hm." Carrie took the dishcloth from Emma's hand and gave her a towel instead. "I'll wash, you dry. It just doesn't seem fair, that's all, you stuck in the *Daadi Haus* caring for your folks with no relief."

"I like how you said that. Caring." Emma's voice held the gentlest of reproaches. "I love them. It's not a burden, not really. Karen comes on Tuesdays so the three of us can have our frolic, and she and John help on Sundays at church, so someone's sitting with Pap on the men's side. And everyone helps clean when church is at our place, so that's no burden either."

She made it sound so reasonable. So straightforward. And maybe she needed it to sound that way, so she could go home again and stay for love, not because God, for reasons of His own, had put rocks in any other path that might be open to her.

Amelia suspected that it wasn't only God who expected Emma to stay home and care for her parents. Everyone did. She was the last remaining unmarried daughter, and had been for enough years that people took it for granted there would be no more courting buggies pulling up in the Stolzfus lane. To everything there was a season, and in the minds of most people in the district Emma's season was past.

There had to be more to a woman's life than that. As she and Emma walked home the way they had come, Amelia pulled up a long stalk of dried grass, its head heavy with seed, and used it as a switch.

There just had to be.

For more, find *The Wounded Heart* at your favorite online retailer, or on my store at moonshellbooks.com!

Glossary

Spelling and definitions from Eugene S. Stine, *Pennsylvania German Dictionary* (Birdboro, PA: Pennsylvania German Society, 1996).

Words used:

Aendi: Auntie

Bann: ban, state of being shunned

batzich: proud

bitte: please

Bobbel: baby

Daadi: Granddad

Daadi Haus: grandfather house

Daed: Dad, Father

Deitch: Pennsylvania Dutch language

denki: thank you; thanks

Dokterfraa: woman who dispenses home remedies

Druwwel: trouble

dummle sich: Hurry up

Eck: corner; tables where the bridal party sits

Es ist zu kalt fer dich.: It's too cold for you.

gakutz: throw up, vomit

genunk: enough

Gmee: congregation; community

Grischdaag, der: Christmas

grossmeenich: proud

Guder Mariye.: Good morning.

gut: good

Hallich Geburtsdaag.: Happy birthday.

Haus: house

Herr, der: the Lord

Hochmut: haughtiness; pride

Isht gut: It's good

ja: yes

Kaffi: coffee

Kamille; Kamilletee: chamomile; chamomile tea

Kapp: woman's prayer covering

leddich: single

Liewi: dear; darling

Mamm: Mom, Mother

Mammi: Grandma

Maad: maid

Meinding, die: shunning, the

meine Freundin: my friends

mupsich: ugly

nei: no

Ordnung: discipline; order

Plappermaul: blabbermouth; chatterbox

plotz: to fall

Rumspringe: running around

Schatzi: little treasure

Schtobbe dich.: You stop it.

schee Meedel: pretty girl

Ungeheier, es: the monster

verhuddelt: confused

Was isht?: What is it?

Was machst?: What's happening?

Was in der Himmelswelt sagst du?: What in heaven's name are you saying?

Was sagst du?: What did you say?

Was tut Sie hier?: What are you doing here?

Wie geht's?: How's it going?

Willkumm: Welcome.

Youngie: young people

Zucker: sugar

Also by Adina Senft

Amish Cowboys of Montana

The Amish Cowboy's Christmas prequel novella
The Amish Cowboy
The Amish Cowboy's Baby
The Amish Cowboy's Bride
The Amish Cowboy's Letter
The Amish Cowboy's Makeover
The Amish Cowboy's Home
The Amish Cowboy's Refuge
The Amish Cowboy's Mistake
The Amish Cowboy's Little Matchmakers
The Amish Cowboy's Wedding Quilt
The Amish Cowboy's Journey

❧

The Whinburg Township Amish
The Wounded Heart
The Hidden Life
The Tempted Soul
Herb of Grace
Keys of Heaven
Balm of Gilead

The Longest Road

The Highest Mountain

The Sweetest Song

The Heart's Return (novella)

Smoke River

Grounds to Believe

Pocketful of Pearls

The Sound of Your Voice

Over Her Head

Glory Prep (faith-based young adult)

Glory Prep

The Fruit of My Lipstick

Be Strong and Curvaceous

Who Made You a Princess?

Tidings of Great Boys

The Chic Shall Inherit the Earth

About the Author

USA Today bestselling author Adina Senft grew up in a plain house church, where she was often asked by outsiders if she was Amish (the answer was no). She holds a PhD in Creative Writing from Lancaster University in the UK. Adina was the winner of RWA's RITA Award for Best Inspirational Novel in 2005 for *Grounds to Believe*, a finalist for that award in 2006 for *Pocketful of Pearls*, and was a Christy Award finalist in 2009 for *The Fruit of My Lipstick*. She appeared in the 2016 documentary film *Love Between the Covers*, is a popular speaker and convention panelist, and has been a guest on many podcasts, including Worldshapers and Realm of Books.

She writes steampunk adventure and mystery as Shelley Adina; and as Charlotte Henry, writes classic Regency romance. When she's not writing, Adina is usually quilting, sewing historical costumes, or enjoying the garden with her flock of rescued chickens.

Adina loves to talk with readers about books, quilting, and chickens!

www.moonshellbooks.com

facebook.com/adinasenft

x.com/shelleyadina

pinterest.com/shelleyadina

bookbub.com/authors/adina-senft

instagram.com/shelleyadinasenft

www.ingramcontent.com/pod-product-compliance
Lightning Source LLC
Chambersburg PA
CBHW031552310726
48973CB00003B/791